About the Author

Keith Fisher was born in Birmingham in 1940 during the bombing. In 1952, he passed the examination, allowing him to go to a grammar school in Smethwick. Although his main area was science, he loved recent history, particularly the lives of ordinary people and the places they worked. Leaving school, he worked in chemical laboratories and did his first degree part-time. He has lived in several countries and finally settled in Australia. This story, although fictitious, comes from his reading about the First World War and stories told by his uncle.

Brummie Twins

Keith Fisher

Brummie Twins

Vanguard Press

VANGUARD PAPERBACK

© Copyright 2024
Keith Fisher

The right of Keith Fisher to be identified as the author of this work has been asserted by him in accordance with the Copyright, Designs and Patents Act 1988.

All Rights Reserved

No reproduction, copy or transmission of this publication may be made without written permission.
No paragraph of this publication may be reproduced, copied or transmitted save with the written permission of the publisher or in accordance with the provisions
of the Copyright Act 1956 (as amended).

Any person who commits any unauthorised act in relation to this publication may be liable to criminal prosecution and civil claims for damages.

A CIP catalogue record for this title is available from the British Library.

ISBN 978-1-83794-273-2

This is a work of fiction. Names, characters, businesses, places, events and incidents are either the products of the author's imagination or used in a fictitious manner. Any resemblance to actual persons, living or dead or actual events is purely coincidental.

Vanguard Press is an imprint of
Pegasus Elliot Mackenzie Publishers Ltd.
www.pegasuspublishers.com

First Published in 2024

Vanguard Press
Sheraton House Castle Park
Cambridge England

Printed & Bound in Great Britain

Dedication

I dedicate this book to my uncle, Percy, who, when I was a boy, told his nephews and nieces interesting stories. He spurred my interest in recent history with stories about Birmingham.

Acknowledgements

I wish to acknowledge my bowling buddy, Andrew Braybrook, who put a lot of effort into making this story more readable.

His Lordship inherited an estate on the border of Birmingham. Just before his father died, he had married. His wife came from landed gentry in Oxfordshire and was henceforth known as 'Her Ladyship'. Within two years, the couple had their first child, Reginald, who was born in 1870. Although his mother breastfed their son, she was not a very caring mother, so a nanny was hired. Her Ladyship wanted her body to get back to normal so she could enjoy her social life. His Lordship would often hold dinner parties and twice a year, he would host a ball.

His Lordship's house had seven bedrooms, a large dining room and a ballroom. Downstairs, there were several rooms for staff and a large kitchen. There was a stable and five outhouses, including a dairy where cows were milked. The farm had seven fields with a coppice in one field. The staff included a manservant who was not really a butler but served His Lordship and conveyed instructions to the other staff. Her ladyship had a maid who saw to her needs, cleaned the bedrooms and helped at dinner parties and balls. The cook was an older widowed lady who had been in the house since she was a young girl. His Lordship regarded her as one of the family but his wife reminded him she was just a servant. There was a groom for the horses, a gardener, a milkmaid who came in the morning and a farmhand who looked after the cows and the ploughing. At harvest time, His Lordship could call on help from the village.

The estate was not large by the standards of the day. The number of staff was also not large compared with other estates. His Lordship's father had been very frugal and had warned his son about the perils of gambling. His Lordship's uncle had worked for the East India Company and had died in India. He had brought back many statues and carvings from India and although he was technically single when he died, the family did not get a penny of his suspected fortune. This taught the family to be cautious with money; 'money had to be earned and saved'.

Reginald, often called Reggie, was a favourite of the cook. When he was young, he would eat anything and as he grew, he especially loved her pastries. The nanny helped in the kitchen but His Lordship hired a scullery maid as he was having an increasing number of parties.

When Reggie was three, he gained a brother who was named Bertrand, later called Bertie. Reggie's birth had been quite smooth but Bertie's birth was more problematic and his mother was not well for a month. Her love for Bertie was diminished compared with her love for Reggie. This manifested itself particularly when the boys had problems or were naughty; Reggie would be loved but Bertie would be scolded. His Lordship noticed and always tried to treat them equally, as he knew that he would have no more children.

Even with the difference in age, these boys were growing up together and rarely quarrelled. They could have had a bedroom each but preferred to share a bedroom. Even comparing their ages, Reggie was stronger and more athletic than Bertie; however, Bertie was more academic and could write at an earlier age than Reggie. Their father enjoyed teaching them to ride, hunt and fish and taught them a work ethic by making them responsible for the grooming of the horses. They had no domestic duties but loved to help the cook in the kitchen. Their mother took very little interest in their lives as she was busy with her own social life, which revolved around afternoon teas, dinner parties and balls. His Lordship tried to involve himself in a lower level of social life but had more interest in his office, which has furnished with an extensive library. His passion was books and he was trying to instil that in his sons, having more effect on Bertie than on Reggie.

At eleven years of age, Reggie was sent to Rugby School as a boarder. His mother was very pleased but his father was thinking that when it was Bertie's time, he would go to a school closer. Reggie was not so good academically but at sports he excelled and his riding skills were getting him good reports. Those reports would prove to be very useful later. He was loving boarding school, even though many of his friends hated it.

At eleven years of age, Bertie was sent to King Edward's School in Birmingham. Although a boarder, because his home was close by, he could go home at the weekend if he wished. He often chose to spend the weekend at home, either tending to the horses or reading his father's books. Academically, he did very well but was not too good at sports, except for riding. School holidays were enjoyed by both boys back at the family estate, with lots of stories shared about school and other pupils. Reggie stayed at school until nearly eighteen but decided not to go to university. They had a military training corps at the school and he decided he would go into the cavalry. His riding skill was duly noted by his instructor and with this man's help, Reggie entered the cavalry as an officer.

During their summer holiday, the boys enjoyed each other's company. Reggie was going to join a cavalry regiment and was enjoying some freedom before he had to go to camp. He had shown how well he could ride and shoot and the regiment was happy to take him. His Lordship was not too happy about this but her ladyship was very proud of Reggie and he was the subject of many of her social events over that summer. Reggie undertook training, then came back home for a final leave before being sent to South Africa.

One Saturday evening, Reggie took Bertie to the stables and made him promise never to tell what he was about to be told. Bertie promised but did not know what he was about to hear.

"I have had my way with the new scullery maid, Sally. I have promised to marry her if she gets pregnant."

Bertie was taken aback. Sally was his age and now he had a secret he could tell no one. Suddenly, his brotherly love had decreased substantially; in fact, he was disgusted. He was lost for words and could not bring himself to let Reggie know what he thought. Bertie was deeply bothered by this news and was glad when Reggie left to join his regiment. Bertie put this development at the back of his mind as he was concentrating on school and had decided to go to university to study law. Reggie was quickly shipped off to South Africa with his regiment to fight the Zulus and now his mother started to think he could be in danger. His father had known this all along, as he was well up to date with developments in the Empire.

Within a couple of months, it was obvious that Sally was pregnant. Bertie wrote to his brother but was not sure how long a letter would take to get to him. He was not even sure whether he would even get the letter. The servants knew that Sally was pregnant and it did not take long before His Lordship also heard the news. He sat in his office and pondered this development. Sally would not name the father but in his mind, there were only two suspects and they were his two sons. The groom was married with children; the gardener was too old and the farmhand was also married. The cook had told him the girl rarely left the house and never went to the village. Both of his sons were capable but Reggie was the prime suspect.

His sworn promise was weighing heavily on Bertie and he vowed that if his father gave Sally the sack, he would break his promise. The cook also knew the name of the father but she had also been sworn to secrecy. His father decided to ignore Sally's pregnancy and let her work until she gave birth. Her ladyship was oblivious to these developments until she went to the kitchen and saw Sally.

She rarely went to the kitchen but wanted a recipe from the cook for one of her friends.

"Get rid of that scullery maid; she is pregnant."

"That girl became pregnant in our house and she will have her baby in this house. Her baby will be a child of my house."

His Lordship spoke loudly and his face was full of anger. He had never spoken to his wife in such a manner and she quickly retreated. His Lordship retired to his office and pondered what he could do about this situation. He knew that Sally's mother had died bearing another child and her father was a labourer living on the border of poverty. He decided that as the gardener was getting old, he would employ Sally's father to help the gardener and the farmhand, thus at least providing him with a steady income. Bertie was a suspect but could he challenge him? For now, he decided to let events take their course and not put pressure on either Sally or Bertie.

Every time Bertie came home from school, he would go to the kitchen first before meeting his parents. He was watching Sally get bigger and bigger and that made him consult some of his father's medical books. Bertie wanted to talk to Sally but he kept his kitchen conversation solely with the cook. He was hoping Sally would not think he was slighting her but he was afraid his anger at Reggie might let him down. He had no reply to his letter to Reggie and was wondering if he should offer to marry Sally.

As time went by, the cook was telling Bertie that Sally was continually tired but tried to do her job. Bertie thought if he married her, she could give up work. Now he was having all sorts of conflicting emotions and he kept telling himself to think rationally. What would his parents say? He did not care what his mother would say but he did not want to give his father a problem. Unknown to Bertie, his father was visiting the kitchen regularly and getting the same reports. Every time Bertie saw Sally, he had visions of Reggie. Maybe Rugby School or his fellow pupils had made him callous; this was not the brother he loved. His thoughts were of when they were young and shared a bedroom; his brother had changed but not for the better.

Bertie was at boarding school when Sally went into labour; her waters broke at two a.m., she called out and the cook came running. She calmed Sally and said she would send for the midwife at six a.m.; if the baby came before that, she would do her best; she had seen several births. At six a.m., the cook went to the stables and luckily, the groom was there. She told him to take a carriage and pick up the midwife as quickly as possible. By the time the midwife arrived, Sally was struggling. The cook had to get breakfast, so she retired to the kitchen. She then prepared the breakfast and put it in the dining room. When she came back to the birth, the midwife was in an excited state – one baby had been born but here was a second on the way. She had never delivered twins before and gave the first baby to the cook to hold. The second baby then appeared and the two ladies were busy for a while with the babies. When the midwife turned back to the mother, she could see that Sally was not breathing. She thumped Sally's chest and tried to lift her head but she was gone.

The cook went to the groom and asked him to fetch the doctor. She had to go back to the kitchen to cry before she went to the midwife and the babies. The midwife would wait for the doctor and then try to find a wet nurse. The babies would need feeding within the day. The cook could not take her eyes off the babies; they were identical girls. The doctor arrived and immediately pronounced Sally dead. He wanted to talk to the house owner, whom he knew very well but His Lordship's man servant said His Lordship was seeing his wife off as she was going to relatives in Oxfordshire. The doctor decided to come back early in the afternoon to talk to His Lordship.

His Lordship was in his office when his man servant introduced the doctor.

"Archibald, to what do I have the pleasure of this surprise visit?"

"Well, I have come with both sad and pleasant news. Your scullery maid died in childbirth but she delivered healthy twins."

His Lordship sat motionless for about thirty seconds and then said, "When did this happen?"

"Early this morning, I would have come to see you sooner but I heard you were sending your wife to her relatives and would not like to send her away on a sad note."

"Where are they now?"

"They are in the room next to the kitchen but Sally is still there."

"I have seen dead bodies before but I have never seen twins."

His Lordship and the doctor went to the room that henceforth would be called the nursery. The cook introduced the lady, who would be the wet nurse. His Lordship could not stop staring at the twins; they were so alike. Finally, he awoke from his trance and asked the wet nurse if he could employ her. She told him she had a small child but she was willing to live there if she could bring her daughter. He told her she could bring her husband if necessary. His Lordship found himself in an elated mood.

Back in his office, His Lordship sat staring out of the window. This new development had thrown him, a large brandy was poured and he toasted the twins. He would have to see those babies again but he must not show too much interest. Now his thought went to twins – were there any in his family? He recalled that one of his aunts had twins and one had died of childbirth. Now he knew the father must be Reggie or Bertie. He would have to register the birth of these girls and he would be their guardian. He told the cook not to bother with his dinner as he was going to Birmingham; she should make sure everyone was well fed, especially the wet nurse.

There was a men's club in Birmingham and he felt that he needed to get out of his house so he could think clearly. He rarely visited the club but knew he could sit quietly and think. He rode to the club and a steward took his horse but his quiet time was anything but. Members were coming to him and wanting to talk. One was congratulating him on having a son in the army in South Africa and another was congratulating him on having a brilliant son at school. In many ways, it was a light relief but he wanted time to think, so after a couple of brandies, he left.

Bertie was at school and knew nothing of these developments. He came home on Friday afternoon and told the cook he was expecting to see Sally. The cook was in tears as she told him Sally was dead, having died in childbirth. Bertie was in tears as he asked why he had not been informed. The cook told him there was so much to do to look after the twins.

"You mean Sally had twin babies?'

"Yes, she had twin girls; would you like to see them?"

Bertie could not comprehend what he was hearing and said, "Of course."

As he entered the nursery, he met the nurse and there in a cot were two very small babies. He had only ever seen a total of two babies in his life and here were two tiny babies together who looked identical. These babies seemed to be staring at him and he could not stop staring at them. This was a new experience. He was lost for words and finally looked at the cook, who smiled. Bertie rushed to her and hugged her. He had last done this when he was young but this was a spur-of-the moment action. He had to leave the nursery to think. How could this happen?

He saddled a horse and rode to the coppice, where he sat for a moment and then shouted the name Sally several times. He heard the echo and hoped it was Sally shouting back. She had given her life to produce two new lives and the father was somewhere in South Africa. His brother had killed Sally and Bertie was cursing himself for not marrying her. He admitted to himself that he had been in love with Sally and was asking himself what would happen next. Sally would have a funeral and he would be there. If his father sent the girls to an orphanage, he would definitely break his promise and tell the truth. His father could be spared a decision if Bertie had the courage to speak up. Now he had to get back to look at those twins.

Sally's funeral was before the Sunday service. Bertie entered the church to find his father already there and he realised his father had to be there as head of the household and as a patron of the church. His Lordship greeted Bertie and said he was glad to see Bertie in the church, all the while thinking about the twin's father; surely, they could not be Bertie's?

Bertie went back to school and all he could think about were the twins. He wrote a long letter to Reggie, much of it impolite. Sally had died as a single mother and because of Bertie's oath, he had said nothing. These twins were bastards and that label would live with them for the rest of their lives. He wished these twins were his, as he thought he would be a better father than his big brother. Bertie wanted to add more but the letter would become too large and the vitriol might get too strong. There was never a reply to this letter.

Every time he saw the twins, he also saw Sally. She was not smiling or talking, just looking at him. It was very unnerving. For a while, it affected his schoolwork but he decided he would have to make enough money to supply the twins with anything they wanted.

His mother returned from Oxfordshire to find they had a nanny for twin babies. She looked at the twins with a disinterested air and then asked the cook who had authorised this change in the routine of the house. The cook replied that it was all His Lordship's doing. Her ladyship went off in a huff and the cook rewarded herself with a broad smile. The nurse asked about her ladyship and the cook told her she was a very strait-laced woman, like her corsets.

Bertie was home from school every weekend; he could not wait to see the twins. He did not know that his father had the same fascination with the twins. Bertie had decided to study law and was investigating how to adopt the twins. He realised he could not act as their father until he had an income. His school reports were so good that he was able to enter Oxford University to read law well before the normal age of undergraduates. His mother was so proud and gave him the addresses of lots of relatives. He hated Oxford and found many of the lectures boring; he had similar thoughts about his relatives. He caught the coach from Oxford to Birmingham at any opportunity. All he wanted to do was see the twins.

The girls had been named Agnes and Elizabeth and Bertie could not tell which was which. His father had devised a means of telling them apart. The nurse would put a red ribbon in Agnes's hair and a blue ribbon in Elizabeth's hair. Bertie did not know this and no one told him. These girls had a small party for their one-year-old birthday, including their grandfather, who was given whisky to celebrate their birthday. He had become a very good gardener after the old gardener retired. Bertie was away in Oxford, celebrating this birthday on his own. He had a couple of drinks and toasted Sally; she was always in his thoughts.

Bertie was finally told how to identify Agnes and Elizabeth by the bows in their hair when the twins were a year old and started to talk. The nurse and her young daughter were trying to teach them to say words. One morning, His Lordship came to the nursery and greeted the twins.

"Olow ward."

"Thank you, Agnes and hello, Elizabeth; I am going to see the horses."

The twins said, "Orses." His Lordship breathed deeply. The nurse apologised; she was trying to get them to say lordship. He said that 'ward' was good enough. He left the nursery and was saying 'ward' to himself; it sounded very good. These girls had a spell on him. The cook had been instructed to buy new clothes as they were growing out of their baby clothes. These twins were costing him practically nothing but in emotional terms, the effect on him was overwhelming.

After one year at Oxford, Bertie decided to transfer to a college in Birmingham. He had heard that Birmingham would get a university in the future but this did not occur until 1900. He told his mother he wanted to be nearer home but she was not impressed. He did not reveal that the real reason was to be close to the twins. By now, he had written several more letters to his brother but there was still no reply. Bertie was very angry with his brother and decided not to write any more letters.

As the twins were growing, Bertie would enjoy reading them stories, some of which he made up, mainly about horses. They loved Uncle 'Ertie; he was so funny. They were soon saying 'lordship and Bertie' but both father and son preferred the shortened first words. The girls were very intelligent and Bertie was soon showing them simple card games like snap. The nurse often took them into the garden and they would chatter to their grandfather, the gardener. He was amazed at how fast they were developing and said they were far more advanced than Sally at a similar age. Later, they liked helping their grandfather with the weeding and pruning. He was helping on the farm and the farm was doing very well, making money.

Bertie was reading law and had a part-time job in a solicitor's office and now he found that he was enjoying the law. This office took on all sorts of cases and sometimes would act for the poor, as one of the partners was a Quaker; he stressed the law was for everyone. Bertie would often sit in court and watch the proceedings with a keen eye on the process. His aim was to become a barrister. Every morning he rose early and was greeted by the twins and a couple of times he caught them up early, watching the milk maid. Agnes said, "We will do that when we get older."

Elizabeth said, "We might need more cows when the two of us do the milking." Bertie was laughing, as he knew from when he played games with them that they worked well together. He had taught them several card games as well as dominoes and draughts. They were very keen players and competitive.

After their fifth birthday, Bertie found two new ponies in the stables. He asked his father about the ponies and was told they were for the girls and that when the ponies were broken in, his father would teach them to ride. He remembered his father had taught him to ride at an early age and show jumping was the only sport he enjoyed and was good at. Bertie had a suspicion that his father loved the twins and now it has been confirmed. He knew that was a good thing, as his father was very much in charge of things and his mother had little say in any aspect of the running of the estate.

As the twins were growing, they called Bertie 'sir' but he decided they should call him uncle. He knew he was their uncle but they did not know. For some reason, they asked about his brother. That put a lump in his throat but he told them his brother was in the army in South Africa.

They started to ask about South Africa, as they thought everyone lived in England. Bertie said that when he came home the next weekend, he would show them the world. He knew his father had a globe and lots of maps, so he would borrow them and show the girls. He asked his father about borrowing the globe and his father said to bring the twins to his study.

One Saturday morning, Bertie took the twins to his father's study. They were wide-eyed as they looked at all the books. His Lordship had decided to let them have his study for half an hour and then he would enter. Bertie was showing them the globe and pointing to England and South Africa. He could see them taking in the information. The globe was a great success and Bertie decided to leave the maps until another time. His Lordship walked in and the twins withdrew their hands from the globe and put them behind their backs.

"Do not mind me. I have some work to do at my desk."

The twins were obviously a bit intimidated, so Bertie said they would come back another time to look at maps. His Lordship was a little disappointed they were leaving so soon but he realised he had surprised them and that they felt uncomfortable. The twins told Bertie they wanted to think about what they had seen. Bertie thought that was an adult response, not the response of two young girls. After this, each time Bertie came home, they wanted to know about other countries.

Agnes asked, "Who owns all these other countries?"

Elizabeth asked, "How do they live and what do they eat?"

Bertie was teaching them geography and at school they were learning the alphabet and how to write letters. Often, he did not know some of the answers to their questions and was asking himself whether he was as advanced as they were at the same age. His first problem was to describe Britain as being surrounded by sea, as the girls had no comprehension of the sea and there was only a small lake on the estate. Bertie thought that perhaps he was going too far in telling them about the world but they were always asking questions. His father was also privy to some of these questions and was marvelling at the progress of the twins. He realised he should not intervene and left it to Bertie. He was fascinated by their fast progress, especially as they often asked questions in unison.

On the estate, these girls were very popular with the staff. They would help the cook in the kitchen and were very good at peeling potatoes. In the stables, they were grooming the horses and would help clean the stables. They helped their grandfather in the garden by weeding and planting. They were slowly expanding the vegetable garden. They both asked (in unison) His Lordship whether she could give her grandfather some vegetables. Of course, he said yes and then started to get sentimental about never having been given the same consideration. At harvest time, they were in the fields helping with the crops.

One cold winter afternoon, Bertie came riding home from Birmingham and put his horse in the stable. As he was leaving the stable, he noticed the twins taking the washing off the line; they seemed to be enjoying themselves. They seemed to be scantily dressed and so Bertie hurried over to them.

"What are you doing in this bitterly cold weather?"

"We enjoy taking these frozen closes; look at the shapes."

"Don't you feel the cold?"

"No and when we get in, cook will give us hot broth."

Bertie left them shaking his head; he was looking forward to a hot broth.

The girls were ten when His Lordship fell sick. The doctor said he had pneumonia and that could be a killer. The doctor could only prescribe breathing menthol, obtained from peppermint oil and rubbing the menthol on his chest. To the surprise of his wife, he said he wanted to see the twins; his wife could leave if she wished but he wanted to talk to the girls. The twins were dressed in their best clothes and curtsied when they entered the bedroom; her ladyship left the room.

"Welcome to my bedroom. I am sick but will get better. You girls can now ride and milk the cows. I want you to do well at school and your other jobs should not interfere with your schoolwork. I expect to get a good report from school in the near future."

The girls were almost in tears, as they loved His Lordship. Together, they both said, "Please, get well." He held out his hand and they both kissed it. He had meant to shake their hands but was touched by the gesture. Reggie had been sent for as he was in England before going back to South Africa. He was a major and was teaching cavalry officers about South Africa. His lectures included the trouble with the Zulus and potential trouble with the Boers.

Reggie arrived and took his horse to the stables. The twins were cleaning one of the stalls as he rode through the door. They saw him and curtsied; they took the reins of his horse. He introduced himself as Bertie's brother. The twins were lost for words; here was a cavalry officer in full uniform. He was very tall and handsome. He smiled, thanked them and walked to the house.

The girls were mesmerised; he was so handsome and when he spoke to them; they were lost for words. His horse was a beautiful thoroughbred and the saddle was the best they had ever seen. They took off the saddle and spent several hours grooming the horse. When they brushed him, the horse stiffened but then relaxed as they continued brushing.

Reggie entered the house and went straight to his father's bedroom. He kissed his mother and went to Bertie, who backed away. Reggie then turned to his father and after a few pleasantries, he said he had something to say.

"I made Sally pregnant and am the father of the twins. I could give many excuses but when I heard she had died, I hoped you would take care of them. If you had disowned them, I would have come back and claimed them. I was so glad you took them into the household."

His mother let out a cry and slumped into a chair. Bertie was now smiling.

"I just met the girls and I cannot tell one from the other. They are beautiful and I see they fit into this estate and you have done a good job."

Everyone was waiting for His Lordship's reaction and when he spoke, it surprised them all.

"At last, I now know that I am their grandfather and you, my dear, are a grandmother."

Her ladyship was still in shock and could not speak.

"This news stays in this room and I don't want the girls to know until you resign from the army. I understand it might kill your career but these girls will be treated as I have always treated them. Let me tell you, I enjoy every time I see them and they are so intelligent. Bertie has been like an uncle to them and now he is their real uncle. Go back to your regiment and I hope to hear good news from South Africa in the future. Now I want to sleep on this news and I am going to defeat this illness."

Everyone left the room and Bertie finally shook Reggie's hand. Their mother retired to her room and only said, "How could you?" Reggie said he would gladly face a hundred Zulus rather than his father. He apologised to Bertie for not replying to his letters but he did not know what to write as he was shocked to hear about Sally's death. Bertie said he should talk to the girls before he left. Reggie was anxious to get back to the barracks but agreed to have tea with his twins.

Bertie went to the stable to find the twins admiring this beautiful horse.

"Uncle Bertie, your brother has the best horse we have ever seen and we love his saddle." They were both saying the same words; that was not new to Bertie.

"We will go to talk to my brother over tea and he might tell you about South Africa."

"How should we call him? Should we say, sir?"

Bertie wanted to call him father but he said they should call him major.

"We have a girl in our class whose father is in the army; he is a sergeant."

"Well, my brother is slightly above him. I will tell you about ranks in the army later."

They entered the dining room with Reggie sitting in an armchair. They curtsied and said in unison, "Good day, Major."

Reggie sat wide-eyed and Bertie explained they often said things together and thought together.

Reggie said, "Please, be seated." That was all he could think of, for they had shocked him. Bertie had to break the ice and so he asked Reggie to tell them about South Africa, as he had shown them Africa on the globe. Reggie relaxed and told them about Zulus and the country where they lived. The twins were mesmerised and could not take their eyes off Reggie. Bertie was thinking he was going to get a lot of questions in the future. They had tea and the girls were about to leave when Bertie said they should kiss Reggie on the cheek as he was leaving to go back to the army. Bertie watched as Reggie was greatly moved by the kisses.

The girls left the room and Reggie said that he had never before seen identical twins; they were so alike and beautiful. When they spoke in unison, they threw him, much like a horse throws a rider. He thanked Bertie for looking after them and apologised for not replying to his letters. There was nothing he could say that would bring Sally back. If his father had sent them to an orphanage, he would have returned to claim them. He was now going back to South Africa with them in his heart and in his mind. Their vision would be something that would spur him on before he retired from the army. There was going to be more trouble in the future in South Africa. He had to be there, as he was so acquainted with the terrain. Reggie said he would talk to his father, then leave; he hoped to be back in a few years.

As Bertie left the room, he saw his nieces hovering near a pillar. They admitted that if Reggie had come from the room, they would have hidden.

"Why are you afraid of my brother?"

"He is a big, strong man," they replied in unison.

"He is not going to hurt you and now I know you want to ask me a question but I have to get back to my office with just one question.

Agnes asked, "Is a major above a sergeant?"

"Yes, we will go to His Lordship's office tomorrow and I will show you all the ranks in the army. Goodbye until tomorrow and I will see you after school."

Bertie thought the girls were not afraid of Reggie; they were more intimidated but that was not in their vocabulary. The funny thing was that Reggie seemed to be equally intimidated by the girls. Bertie was preparing himself for an onslaught of questions. He thought he could concentrate on the army but these girls' trains of thought often took surprising turns. They seemed to have a knack for taking an answer and using it to go into a new area. He was always astounded at the direction's conversation could take.

His Lordship rallied and the next day he was well enough to go to his office. He had to get well, as he was now a real grandfather.

Bertie met the girls after school and they went to His Lordship's office. Bertie showed them a plan of the army structure, from the private to the field marshal. They identified that a major was somewhere in the middle and a sergeant was much lower. Then they asked how Reggie could become a general. As they were asking the question, His Lordship entered the office and he heard the question.

They saw His Lordship and in unison, apologised for being in his office. He told them they would not disturb him, as he just wanted to look at some papers. They were to continue asking Bertie questions; he would not be disturbed. He was staring at them whenever they were not looking his way and he was mentally answering their questions. His Lordship had never been in the army but he was very well versed in the army's structure and operations. He knew less about South Africa and when the girls departed, he would be consulting his atlases. At various stages, he wanted to tell the twins that Reggie was their father but he had put the restriction on them knowing, so he had to keep quiet.

Slowly, the twins took over the duties of the milkmaid, so His Lordship employed her in the kitchen to help the aging cook. One morning, he was up early to watch the twins milk the cows before going to school. He watched the girls call out names and the cows would line up to be milked. He could not believe what he was seeing. He let them go to school and all day he realised he would have to ask questions.

When they came from school, he found them in the stables and asked how they milked the cows. They told him each cow had a name and some cows would go to Elizabeth and some to Agnes. They said that they knew the calm cows and the fidgety ones. His Lordship shook his head and went back to his office to talk to Bertie. Bertie told him they had names for the horses and they had told him they had problems with the chickens. His Lordship laughed and said he should just hand over the farm to them. Henceforth, His Lordship paid more attention to milk and egg production and found both were increasing.

They were about twelve when Bertie joined them on their way from school. They were doing very well at school and were far more advanced than the other pupils. The teacher told Bertie she had to stop them from answering all the questions and when allowed to answer; they did it in unison. This day they were laughing and Bertie asked about the joke.

Agnes said, "The teacher wants to split us up in the classroom, so we don't collaborate." A word Bertie had told them.

Elizabeth said, "She could put us in different rooms, and we would still know what the other had said."

Bertie was intrigued and wanted to do an experiment. He asked his father whether he would participate and His Lordship was very happy to oblige. Bertie explained that he would ask Agnes a question and His Lordship would ask Elizabeth the answer, not telling her the question. His Lordship would ask Elizabeth a question and Bertie would ask the answer; they would be in separate rooms.

Bertie asked whether Reggie was older or younger than him. Agnes replied, 'older' and Elizabeth told His Lordship, 'Older'. His Lordship did not know the question but asked Elizabeth the name of the cook. She answered 'Violet' and Agnes told Bertie 'Violet'. They got together and they confirmed that they knew what each other said. When the twins left the room, His Lordship was excited and said that maybe they should let some medical people know about these results. Bertie persuaded his father to keep this a secret, as the twins might come under scrutiny. He also warned against telling his mother, as she might want them as a sort of entertainment sideshow at her social gatherings. His father admitted that he never talked to his wife about the twins.

The twins left school at fourteen and then worked full time on the farm. His Lordship asked whether they would like to do other things besides farming. Their answer was that they wanted to try everything on the farm and wanted to know how to keep the 'books'. His Lordship told them they were called accounts and he would happily sit down to teach them the process. He would buy them a book each and start them writing about all the assets of the estate and how they were managed. Privately, he was very happy that he would be close to the girls every day.

Reggie was writing regular letters from South Africa to Bertie and his father. His Lordship told the twins and the big news was that he had been promoted to Colonel. That started a conversation about the army and what Reggie was doing. His Lordship was enjoying these conversations and the twins told him that Bertie was nice and quiet but they were excited by Reggie. He could understand fifteen-year-old girls being excited by a handsome army officer. They should know Reggie was their father and it was tormenting him that they could not know about their father until he had Reggie's permission. Reggie was involved in chasing Zulu uprisings and keeping a close eye on the Boers, so it was not the time to ask him to reveal his true relationship with the twins.

Her ladyship was spending a lot of time in Oxford. She had met a general who knew Reggie and was full of praise of Reggie and said he was a born leader of men. She did not understand the strategy and the politics of the situation but she loved the idea of her eldest son as a hero. His Lordship told her that the younger son was also doing very well in his profession but she did not want to know about Bertie. She had forgotten that Reggie was the father of the twins. His Lordship was not worried by her absence and in fact, he enjoyed himself when she was away.

The girls were more or less running the farm and when market days came, they would go with His Lordship. They would inspect the cattle and horses. His Lordship rarely sold but he was often buying more stock. The farmers and auctioneers knew these girls and were always polite to them, even though they actually wished that the girls would go away. They were too shrewd. If His Lordship was bidding on cattle or horses and about to pay too much, they had a secret sign to stop him from bidding. They had a different sign at each market and His Lordship had to remember the new sign. Often, he would have bid more but had the good sense to obey the twins. He would come home and have a couple of whiskies with his son while telling him what had taken place at the market. These girls had silently taken control.

When the girls were sixteen, one of their school friends was getting married and the twins were invited to be bridesmaids. Bertie reminded them that they should not outshine the bride.

"Uncle Bertie, we know the rules," they said.

"She is our friend and we would do nothing to hurt her," said Agnes and Elizabeth.

Bertie had been rebuked and he was smiling to himself with the knowledge that these girls were becoming confident and outspoken. After the wedding, Bertie asked them whether they had met any interesting young men.

"The ones we met were immature and knew nothing. I tried talking to one about South Africa and did not know where it was."

Elizabeth chimed in, "They did not know what Zulus were and no one knew how to get to Australia. All the boys we met were hopeless."

Agnes said she asked one boy if Queen Victoria was married and he said he thought she was. "We gave up on them all."

Bertie was shaking his head at all of this when they surprised him by asking why he was not married.

"No one has ever asked me."

In unison, they said, "That is not the way it is done; you have to ask the lady."

"Oh, you mean I have been getting it all wrong?"

They were all laughing when His Lordship entered the room and asked about the joke. Agnes told him that Bertie was waiting for a lady to ask him to marry her.

"Well, that may be the way in the future."

"Sorry, sir, we live now and not in the future," said Elizabeth.

Now His Lordship had been rebuked.

Bertie was trying to encourage them to get off the farm more often and invited them to his office. His Lordship was lamenting the fact that he could not introduce them to society. He was sure they would be a match for any young man with a title. He started to go to more dinner parties with his wife. There was an ulterior motive; he wanted to see if any of the young men could match his granddaughters. He was disappointed that not one young man he met could match them with knowledge or intellect. Bertie was also looking at young men and finding them all unworthy of the twins.

The twins were going to some functions outside the farm but they all seemed to be women's meetings. At one meeting, a young lady was speaking about votes for women when the meeting was broken up by the police; the speaker was charged with a breach of the peace. The girls were shocked and immediately went to talk to Uncle Bertie. They described the meeting and asked for Uncle Bertie's help.

"Where was the meeting?"

"At the church hall," they answered in unison.

Where are there any men present?"

"We did not see any."

"Was there any violence?"

"No, we were all in shock."

"Give me the name and address of this young lady and I will talk to her."

"Please, Uncle Bertie, you should represent her in court; we don't think she can pay."

"I am not worried about her paying but justice has to be seen to be done. If what you have told me is true, we should win this case without you having to attend court."

Bertie knocked on the door of the address he had been given and was greeted by an older man. Bertie introduced himself and explained that he wanted to talk to Lisa; he said her father could be present. Her father said her older sister, Elsie, would be present. Bertie met them in the living room and told Lisa he might be able to represent her in her coming court case. Lisa was almost in tears, so Elsie took over.

Bertie asked if Elsie was present at the meeting. When she said she had not been present, Bertie apologised and said she could not help her sister's case. He was upset he had to be so blunt, as he liked Elsie.

"Did you resist arrest and did you swear at the police?"

"No, I was in shock and they had me in handcuffs before I could speak. The whole audience was in shock."

"Did you say anything at the police station?"

"No, I was still in shock and all I said was that I was innocent of any crime."

"At the meeting, did you say anything about the crown or the government?"

"No, I just started to explain what the vote could do for women and I was only speaking for five minutes when the police came and I stopped as they entered."

"Are you a member of a movement?"

"No, I learned about voting rights in the library."

Bertie thought she must have had some tutoring but she was naive and he found that he rather fancied her sister. He said that he would represent her and that he needed no payment. Later, the twins asked if they could be in court; Bertie told them that was all right as long as they kept quiet. Now he had begun work to prepare for the case.

The police case was that they had disrupted an illegal meeting and had arrested the speaker at the meeting. Bertie listened to their evidence. He saw that the magistrate was a man that he knew to be fair. The police sergeant was asked what was wrong with a group of women discussing things that affected them. Bertie asked if there had been a complaint and if so, they should name the complainant. The magistrate was watching the police case fall apart and to stop further embarrassment, he halted the proceedings and threw out the case.

Now Bertie was the twin's hero. He invited Lisa, Elsie and the twins to lunch and explained that he did not normally do that with defendants. Bertie was going to be the only man with four women and he thought the best course of action he could take was to mainly listen. The twins were full of praise for Bertie and he was pleased to notice that Elsie was also impressed. Lisa was very grateful and said she would be more careful in the future. He allowed the ladies to do all the talking and finally asked Elsie what she did for a living. She told him she was a dressmaker. The twins were watching Bertie and knew him well enough to see his interest. They proceeded to formulate a plan. They talked His Lordship into having a small party with young people present. Her ladyship was away, so they invited Lisa, Elsie, and their friend, who had recently married, along with her husband. They warned His Lordship that this company might not be to his liking but he should hear the opinions of the younger generation.

He was left shaking his head; these girls could twist him around their little fingers. Of course, Bertie was invited.

His Lordship duly put on a dinner for eight and sat back to watch the proceedings. At first, the guests seemed intimidated by the regal surroundings but the twins did a good job of starting the conversations. They asked their friend about married life and talked to her husband about his job. In turn, Lisa and Elsie were asked why they were not married; Bertie had to interject, saying those things were personal. That started Elsie talking and she was saying she had not met the man for her. Lisa said she had not met any men that interested her. By the end of the dinner, everyone was talking freely and obviously, the wine helped. Later, His Lordship told Bertie that was the best dinner party he had ever organised and then subsequently confessed that the twins had organised it.

Bertie was inviting Elsie out to lunch as she worked near his office. He had taken her to a play and was often in her company. The twins were thrilled; Bertie was walking out with Elsie. They were hoping to be bridesmaids at a future wedding, as they really loved their uncle Bertie and thought Elsie was a good match. Now they had to put their match-making skills in another direction. They visited Bertie's office to look over the young clerks. They found one, Richard, who was quite smart and reasonably good-looking. He could be suitable for Lisa. The twins discussed how they could bring Richard and Lisa together. The answer was another dinner party.

Bertie was told to bring Richard to a dinner party they would talk His Lordship into having. Bertie was thinking one of the girls was interested in Richard but which one? Of course, he was wide of the mark, as the twins had other ideas. His Lordship said he would wait until his wife went to Oxford. Bertie warned him there would be nine people attending and his father's response was that the table sat twelve, so the more the merrier.

The twins made up the seating plan and Richard was seated next to Lisa. Bertie was, of course, seated next to Elsie and the twins were either side of His Lordship. Again, the twins led the conversation by asking Richard what he did for a living. That started a long discussion of the law, with Bertie only having to correct some minor misunderstandings. His Lordship was saying nothing, only absorbing the conversation. Listening to the young people speaking, he could only compare this with dinner parties he had been to with his wife, where the focus was talking about debutantes, horse jumping events and other rubbish. This was more like real life.

The twins were watching Richard and Lisa, who seemed to be talking freely to each other, which was a good sign. Their other friend and her husband were joining in the conversation and the wife asked about Bertie's elder brother. His Lordship perked up but he was going to let Bertie do the talking. Actually, Bertie only said a few words and then the twins took over. In unison, they told the guests about the South African situation and what Reggie was doing. His Lordship and Bertie sat back and listened. Richard brought up a good point and asked why Britain had an army in South Africa. Now Lisa joined in and talked about the Empire. Bertie knew she had learned a lot about the subject. Finally, the dinner party broke up and Bertie was going to take them all home in the carriage.

After they had left, the twins asked His Lordship whether they had behaved correctly and they hoped he was not bored. He was elated and said he enjoyed the evening; he really wanted to say that this dinner was the best company that he had had for some time. When Bertie returned, he could express his real opinion. They sat and had a drink and His Lordship said it was like entering a new world. These young people had ideas and expressed them differently. He felt he was hearing a new approach to the world. Bertie said he was going to marry Elsie but to keep it quiet for a while. His father told him he had made an excellent choice. Bertie thought about his choice. He would marry either of the twins or even both but he recognised that was not possible.

After a few weeks, the twins found out that Richard and Lisa were walking out. Now they had to plan for when Bertie would get married. However, personally, they still found no young men that interested them. His Lordship was regularly sharing his office with the twins and they were borrowing his books. He had many books, some acquired from his father but when he went to Birmingham, he was always buying books. The twins were often with him, advising him on what books to buy. Mr Dickens was their favourite and His Lordship found himself buying up the whole collection. His wife had looked at some of these new books and disapproved of his reading tastes. His Lordship had a problem as he could not tell her what he really was thinking; it was not going to be at all to her liking.

The season's passed. The twins were approaching eighteen and Bertie was soon to be married. His mother constantly said 'dress maker' in a very derogatory way; she had forgotten her eldest and favourite son had bedded a scullery maid. She was only going to be attending the wedding under duress. Actually, Bertie did not care but his father was putting his foot down and insisted on his wife's attendance. He liked Elsie and was glad his favourite son, Bertie, had found a worthy wife. What was tormenting him was that the twins still did not know he was their grandfather.

Finally, His Lordship wrote to Reggie and asked whether he could tell the twins the identity of their father. He wanted to announce it on their eighteenth birthday. Reggie's response was that he was glad to let them know about their father and it could not affect his career, as there was soon to be war with the Boers.

The wedding was timed to coincide with the twins' eighteenth birthday. His Lordship was wrestling with a problem: whether to make the announcement of Reggie as the father at the wedding or before the wedding? Bertie said that he thought about it before the wedding and that his father should tell the twins in private so that if they wanted to keep it secret, they could. Several days later, His

Lordship asked the twins to come to his office and asked them to sit. He then told them Reggie was their father and they rushed him, knocking him into his chair. They were hugging and kissing him and all three of them had tears in their eyes. In unison, they announced that they had suspected that Reggie was their father but that was not important; what was important was that they could now call His Lordship 'grandfather' but not in public. His Lordship was left wondering why he had waited so long.

Bertie was duly married with his mother in attendance; Richard was his best man; and of course, the twins were bridesmaids. There was a small reception on the estate. Bertie had refused to invite his relatives from Oxford but the gardener and the cook, as well as the twin's married friend and her husband, were invited. Elsie's parents felt a little out of place but Lisa set them at ease by telling them she had been at dinner parties in this great house.

His Lordship privately told Bertie that the announcement of Reggie as the twins' father had gone very well and it was one of the best days of his life. Bertie knew that the girls were fully running the estate and he talked to his father about other land holdings that his father held on the edge of Birmingham. The city was growing and industry was bringing more labour in from the surrounding countryside. These workers needed housing and Bertie was keen on using some of this land to meet the demand and produce rental income. This area would become important later.

Her ladyship was generally not happy with the wedding but found herself rather admiring her granddaughters. These girls had a presence and they conducted themselves as young ladies should. None of her friends or relatives were at the church or reception but her attitude towards the twins was softening and she began to think that they would benefit from being introduced to 'real' people soon.

His Lordship was enjoying the reception and had to dance with each of his granddaughters. They spoke to him as a normal couple having a dance and he was wishing he were forty years younger. Suddenly he was feeling his age and there was nothing he could do about it. He was watching Bertie dancing with Elsie and Richard dancing with Lisa and he was hoping to have another wedding in his house. The only problem and he acknowledged it as a large one, was that his granddaughters had no prospective husbands.

The news from South Africa was that war was imminent. Reggie had been promoted to Brigadier and promotion was accelerated due to his knowledge of South Africa. His Lordship was sharing Reggie's letters with the twins, as there was nothing private that could not be shared with them. On the home front, Elsie was pregnant and that excited the twins the most. Bertie was not his calm self and the twins had to constantly tell him not to worry. In his mind's eye, he was seeing Sally all over again and this vision of her was frightening him intensely. He could not tell Elsie or the twins; the only one he could talk to was the cook, Violet. Violet admitted that Sally had told her that Reggie was the father but she had also been sworn to secrecy. She told Bertie that the birth of twins had been too much for Sally but Elsie was a strong girl and Bertie should not be worried. Bertie knew about death in childbirth and he remained worried.

The twins were looking forward to the birth of Elsie and Bertie's baby and the imminent wedding of Richard and Lisa. They had told their grandfather that when Richard and Lisa were married, the reception should be held on the estate. Her Ladyship was asking about the reception. His Lordship's answer was that this couple had met on the estate and he was responsible, even though secretly he knew it was all due to the twins.

Elsie went into labour two days before the wedding and that had the twins in a tizz. For once, they each had a different idea about what they should do. Agnes wanted to be with Elsie and Elizabeth wanted to adjust their bridesmaid's dresses. They decided to separate and do their own thing. This was the first but not the last time they decided to go separate ways.

Agnes found Bertie in a very anxious state. She told him there was nothing he could do but stay out of the way. The doctor and the midwife were in attendance and they allowed Agnes to be in the room, just in case she was needed. Elsie's labour was quite short and Agnes witnessed the baby being born. She had previously seen a foal being born but this was special and she had tears running down her cheeks.

Elizabeth had gone to talk to Lisa and they spoke about her sister's labour. Elizabeth had reasoned that if they could not see the birth, it was better to do something useful. She and Lisa sat down and talked about the procedure for the wedding. Elizabeth had been through it at Bertie's wedding. They were discussing the dresses when Elizabeth suddenly stood up and said the baby had been born. There were tears streaming down Elizabeth's face. She apologised to Lisa and said she had to get back to the house.

The baby was a boy and the twins were celebrating like it was one of theirs. They were hugging and kissing Bertie and telling him he would soon see his son. His Lordship was celebrating a third grandchild and this was a boy. The twins kissed their grandfather and told him they knew a boy was very special and they would regard him as their brother. His Lordship became emotional and excused himself by saying he needed a whisky. Her Ladyship was thanking Bertie for giving her a grandson. The twins were smiling, knowing they could never win their grandmother's heart.

Two days later, the wedding went smoothly and Bertie attended but Elsie was resting. The twins were asking Bertie about the baby and whether he had a name yet. Bertie said it was Elsie's choice. His mother overheard the conversation and forcefully interjected, telling Bertie the name was his choice. He said times were changing and Elsie had gone through the pain and a small thing like a name would be her choice. Her ladyship went off in a huff and the twins were smiling at Bertie. They were not going to make a comment, as maybe they would be overheard.

The reception was a great success and the twins' other grandfather, the gardener on the estate, was having a good time. He did not yet know about His Lordship being the other grandfather. They had kept it secret, although they had toyed with and discussed the idea of telling him. His Lordship was greeting everyone but his wife was staying in the background as none of these people were 'her kind' but she had to be polite. Bertie was talking to Richard and told him he could have the week off and stay in Bertie's flat above the office. Bertie had been told by his father that he should live on the estate and that there was no need for the flat in Birmingham. The twins also wanted Bertie and Elsie to live on the estate.

The twins were constantly looking in on Elsie and the baby; he fascinated them and they talked endlessly about a name for the baby. Elsie liked Richard but she also had a new brother-in-law named Richard. Agnes suggested Benjamin but Elizabeth did not like that name. Elsie said that as the mother, she liked the name and would ask Bertie if that name was acceptable. Bertie, of course, said the name was acceptable. Elizabeth said, "How about Jonathon for the second name?" and that was also acceptable to Bertie and Elsie. These discussions highlighted the way that the twins were growing and starting to have some different ideas but generally they were in agreement and in unison.

The news from South Africa was that war was imminent. Reggie wrote that the Boers were excellent riders and shooters. He had watched them over many years and thought the British army underestimated them as a fighting force. He had relayed his concerns to several generals but the high command seemed to be ignoring his advice, despite the fact that he had been in South Africa a long time and knew the people and the terrain. He wrote that his future letters might be censored and they may not get through, so he was wishing everyone good health, particularly his father, mother and the twins.

One day, her ladyship asked her husband, what were the twins doing? She had no interest in them for such a long time that His Lordship was puzzled as to why she suddenly took an interest. His reply was blunt: "running the estate."

"Why is Bertie not running the estate? How can you leave it to two girls?"

"Bertie has a profession and now a family. I doubt whether he could do a better job than Agnes and Elizabeth. They report everything to me and I can find no fault in what they do. I used to go to the market to buy and sell livestock but these two girls are shrewder and I am sure they get better prices both buying and selling. I know Reggie will take over when he eventually resigns his commission but he will have two excellent teachers in his daughters."

"Daughters teaching their father. What is the world coming to?" With that, she left the room in a huff.

His Lordship was sitting at his desk smiling; he realised how his wife was out of tune with the family. He wondered how often she actually saw her grandchildren. The twins reported to him every day and they would have a discussion for at least one hour. He would also take time every day to visit the nursery to talk to his grandson. Of course, it was a one-way conversation but His Lordship enjoyed telling Benjamin all about the family. He was also refreshing his own memory while he was talking. Generally, he sent Elsie or the nurse away so he could have a private conversation. He met Bertie in the evening and was continually complimenting him on his bouncing baby boy. They would have a drink before supper and her ladyship would often take her supper in her room. In her absence, conversation could be lively; when she was present, the talk was more subdued.

Benjamin was approaching his first birthday and it should have been a happy time but there was no news from Reggie in South Africa, it appeared that the war was not going well and some towns were besieged. Bertie was telling the twins to be positive when they talked to their grandfather. They were trying their best but their other grandfather was sick and they were spending their spare hours nursing him. His Lordship asked his doctor to see the other grandfather and the news was not good; the man had lung problems and was not going to last more than a few months.

Life went on. The baby Benjamin was now saying a few words and the twins, along with his grandfather, were talking to him every day. There was some bright news, as

Elsie thought she might be pregnant again; it was a false alarm but her sister Lisa was pregnant. Bertie's law practice was doing very well and Richard was his senior clerk and office manager. Bertie was also involved in the formation of the University of Birmingham. The twins were very proud of their uncle and would sing his praises, particularly when her ladyship was present. His Lordship loved these occasions but gradually his health was failing and he could not sit long at the supper table.

The twins were praying their father would come home safe. They talked to each other about the future. If their father came home, he would automatically take over the estate; that was his right. They would help him but his say would be 'law'. They were already taking care of sick people and seeing babies born, so maybe they should become nurses. This became firm in their minds when their mother's father died. They had nursed him till the end and even neglected the estate a little. His Lordship understood and he enlisted Bertie's help for a time. Bertie admitted that even though the twins were overseeing the estate part-time, they were still doing a better job than he could.

Finally, there was a letter from Reggie. He had not been locked up in a besieged city but instead had taken his brigade into the country and tried to play the game and fight like the Boers. They would attack swiftly and then retreat. They would live off the land and if the Boers attacked, they would retreat to the south, a more friendly country. He had help from some Zulus who were opposed to the Boers. The letter was positive and ended by telling everyone not to worry but the war would not come to an end soon.

    The twins were very happy with that letter and they told His Lordship they would hold a party. He was to leave it all to them; they were running the show. They planned the event when her ladyship was in Oxford so as not to upset her. Richard, Lisa's husband, knew an entertainer who could sing, play the piano and also the accordion. The twins said they could not sing but Lisa had a good voice and she would sing a few songs. Elsie told Bertie her sister could sing and they could all sing along with her. Bertie admitted he was not a singer but he would join in if others were singing. The twins decided that they would break with tradition and there would not be a formal supper but there would be food laid out on a long table and guests could pick what they wanted. His Lordship watched this process with fascination; it was so different from a normal dinner party that he loved the way it worked. The twins brought him a plate and said that if he wanted more food, he should let them know. This was all so different and he was fascinated watching the guests sit wherever they liked and also pick the food they wanted.

    The entertainment and the singing started. Bertie came to his father and asked whether it was too loud.

    "I am sitting here and I can't believe what I am seeing and hearing. This is so different; I cannot help but enjoy it. The problem for me is that I am too old to join in the singing and dancing. I have been to so many stuffy dinner parties and I thought that was all there was but now I am seeing things differently. My granddaughters know how to put on a party."

Bertie had to agree that this was very different and his wife and son were enjoying the festivities. The twins came to His Lordship and asked if it was too loud. He hugged them and said they could make it louder if they liked; he did not care. As they left him, he had a tear in his eye. He wondered how long he would live to see this excitement again. He was really wondering how long he could be with his granddaughters.

The twins had decided on nursing as a career and they asked Bertie how they could learn about nursing. He found there was a course at the Birmingham Technical Institute and said he would investigate the timing of the course. They told their grandfather about going to college to learn about nursing but promised they would still run the estate. He was glad they were thinking of a profession more suited to ladies but he felt that they could probably run an estate better than any man. There would be no opportunity for them to do that.

The twins had to ride to Bertie's office in the city to stable their horses. From there, it was a short walk to the Technical Institute. They entered the class to find they were in a group of sixteen girls. The first nursing course was a preliminary course and they knew more than the other girls, who were much younger. The teacher and the other students were surprised when the twins spoke in unison but they all soon got used to their speech.

Bertie had enrolled them as his wards, so any administrative or enrolment questions would come to him. He did not want anyone prying into their background, as he knew they would stand out. One thing the twins learned early on in the course was that there were many industrial accidents in a city like Birmingham. There was also large industry in the surrounding areas, particularly in the Black Country. The lecturer showed them the accident records in one hospital and there were a great many broken arms and legs, severed hands and fingers and many burns. They had no idea the industry could be so dangerous.

They asked their uncle Bertie if they could ride to the Black Country. They lived on the other side of Birmingham, in a rural area. He said he would not let them go alone and he would arrange an afternoon off work and ride with them. They arranged to meet at his office if the weather was good; if not, they would plan another day. He said they would ride along the Hagley Road and head into Smethwick. They would see foundries and coal mines in Oldbury, the next town. He said they would then turn back along the Dudley Road back into Birmingham.

The twins were fascinated by the sights. They were astounded at the number of pubs, starting with the King's Head. They had pubs in their area but had never really noticed them. Their next shock was the smoke and smell. There were fumes belching from every factory. They asked Bertie where the workers lived; he told them they would not go there and would only stick to the main road. On their way back, they saw the canal and the railway line.

They stopped to watch the barges being pulled by horses and saw a train. They told Bertie they had never been on a train or a barge. He said that he could arrange a trip on a barge to Oxford to visit relatives. As soon as he said, 'visiting relatives,' he thought it was probably not a good idea until their status was known.

The twins returned to the estate with lots to discuss; they realised they had led sheltered lives. Bertie was not keen on a barge trip but promised a train trip. They thought that if they were going to be nurses, they would be nursing ordinary people but they realised that they knew none except their deceased grandfather, the groom and the farm labourer. They determined that they had to get off the estate more often and see some sights. They first went to His Lordship's office to consult his maps; they wanted to look at the locations of train lines and canals. Looking at the maps, there was a canal near Alvechurch, which was a good ride. They decided to leave the train journey to their uncle but they would investigate the barges on their own.

One morning, they told their grandfather they were going for a long ride. All he could say was "take care." He wondered whether a normal grandfather would be worried but he had full faith in his granddaughters; he had taught them to ride and knew they were excellent riders. They were not riding into the city, so he assumed there would be no problem. Most women rode side-saddle but these girls had split skirts and rode like men. He often watched them with horses and they seemed to be able to talk to horses.

The girls rode to Alvechurch and found the canal; there was a barge parked and so they dismounted. They walked over to the bargee and asked together if they could look at his barge. He stood open-mouthed until his wife pushed him out of the way.

"Can you please repeat that request? My husband is still in shock."

They repeated the phrase and the bargee's wife told them she loved their spoken English but two ladies speaking in unison was something new. She was well educated and admitted that she fell in love with a bargee and her family had disowned her. They plied their trade from Birmingham to London and generally carried coal and iron products from Birmingham and on the way back, they had goods from the continent and India. The bargee's wife was intrigued by the twins riding like men; she had only ever seen ladies riding side-saddle. She was very happy to show them the living quarters. There was a living room, a bedroom with two beds and a kitchen with a portable charcoal stove. The lady said they took the stove on the deck to cook; some barges had been set on fire with faulty stoves. She showed them the cargo and her husband still seemed to be in shock. The twins thanked her and offered money for the tour.

"No, thank you; it was a pleasure to meet you. Most bargees will tell you they are poor but we have a good life and you will become famous when word spreads among the other bargees. The pleasure has been all mine."

As they rode off, the bargee was shaking his head and his wife was waving goodbye. They had a pleasant ride back to the estate and plenty to talk about. Firstly, they reported to His Lordship and then went to look at more maps. The number of the barge was put in their diary, for they wanted to see that lady again. When Bertie learned of their trip, he said there was a basin quite near his office. They told him they enjoyed the ride and saw many more things than barges. The twins were becoming more vigilant. Whenever they went into Birmingham, they visited the basin, looking for a barge with the number they had written. They also rode to Winson Green to look at barges. They had no problems on their rides; people just stood and stared.

Bertie organised a train trip and Elsie was going to take Benjamin. They would catch the train at Snow Hill and travel to Bewdley. Much of the trip would be through the Black Country and that excited the twins. Elsie admitted she had never seen this side of Birmingham. Bertie took the carriage to Birmingham and left it with Richard. Elsie had not seen her sister for some time and although Lisa was heavily pregnant, she asked whether she could come. Bertie was a bit reluctant but the twins assured him they would know what to do if Lisa went into labour. The twins had a private discussion and in one way they were hoping Lisa would not go into labour but they also had a sneaking hope they would deliver a baby.

Snow Hill Station was a wonder for the twins. There were several trains in the station and the noise was deafening. They found an empty compartment and everyone enjoyed comfortable seats. The engine blew its whistle and Benjamin started to shout, showing his childish enjoyment. The train travelled through Smethwick and Oldbury where they saw the mines and blast furnaces. There were chemical works giving off a foul smell but whereas Elsie was not enjoying the experience, the twins loved every minute, Benjamin also loved the trip; he was continually bouncing up and down. The train stopped at Kidderminster and they saw textile factories. These were factories in a rural setting and that intrigued the twins. Bertie had to tell them this was the centre of carpet making. Some of the mill owners were his clients.

The group alighted the train at Bewdley and Bertie said it was a short walk to the river. He asked if Lisa was up for a walk and she told him a walk was better than just sitting. The twins thought this was a beautiful little town, enhanced by the River Severn. There was a pub on the side of the river with a place to sit. Bertie took the twins into the bar to order lunch. They had never been in a pub before and when they spoke in unison; the bar became quiet. The barman looked at them in astonishment and they asked what refreshments were available. He was speechless and Bertie told the twins to leave it to him.

Lunch outside the pub, facing the river, was a delight for the whole party; Benjamin was enjoying himself, looking at the river and the fishermen. Lisa found it more comfortable to stand at the rail, looking at the river, rather than sit on the bench. Bertie was worried and the twins told him to calm down. Elsie was telling Bertie they should do this again and she suggested Stratford-upon-Avon. Bertie realised he would have to organise his work schedule. The trip back to Birmingham had Lisa and Elsie asleep and Benjamin was very quiet as he was obviously tired. The twins were excited and always seeing new sights; Bertie was watching and smiling at the comments the girls were making. These girls were different from any ladies he knew. They were taking an interest in things he thought most other ladies would ignore.

Arriving back on the estate, the twins were reporting to His Lordship. He said he had never been to Bewdley but had been to Worcester many times to see the races and the cricket. The twins started to ask him about cricket but he apologised as he was tired and would tell them about the game at a later date. The twins left the bedroom and they were sorry they had overexcited their grandfather; they would have to be careful in the future. Bertie had told them not to tax His Lordship's strength.

The news from South Africa was that the besieged towns had been liberated and the word Mafeking was on many lips. The British Army now had the upper hand and was pouring troops into South Africa. The twins had no news about their father but were buoyed by the news of the army winning, whereas before, they seemed to be losing. They were again consulting maps in His Lordship's office. Bertie told the twins he hoped this war would finish soon, as his father was not improving and he wanted Reggie to come home before his father died. The twins had seen their other grandfather die but in some ways, this was different. They told Bertie to take heart, while they were also privately thinking the worst.

News was coming that a peace treaty had been signed and Bertie was telling the twins it could be a long time before their father came home. Reggie resigned his commission as soon as the war was over and was home within two months. Reggie told Bertie he was upset with the British army's tactics. They were burning Boer farms, putting women, children and old people in camps. These camps were horrible places, with little food or water and no compassion. His brigade had been in the veld and often had to attack Boer farms but they only took what they needed and always left the farmers with enough to keep their families from starving. He made sure the troops did not burn farmhouses. Now that he was back, he wanted to make sure no Englishman starved; he had seen enough starvation. Bertie called him an idealist.

The twins put on a party for their returning father; they had previously been greeting him with lots of kisses and hugs. He was confronted with many people he did not know (for he had been in South Africa for so long) except Bertie. He had not previously met Elsie and Benjamin. There was a table covered with food and everyone was taking a plate and sitting where they wanted to sit. This was different. Bertie explained the process to Reggie and introduced most of the guests. His Lordship wanted to be present but he was in his bedroom, too sick to join the party. Her ladyship took one look at the proceedings and went straight back to her room. Everyone treated Reggie with respect, except his daughters, who were coming and kissing him every five minutes. Bertie was telling his brother to lose his reserve, as these girls had waited a long time for this party. Reggie smiled and said this was all new to him but he could handle it.

Bertie took the twins on one side and said they should approach their father individually so he could know their characters.

"We both have the same character."

"Well, give him a chance to deal with you one-on-one."

"Uncle Bertie, you have a good idea; we will give it a try."

The next morning, after breakfast (just Reggie and his mother), they went to His Lordship's bedroom. There, Reggie and his mother met the twins, who said they would have breakfast later as the first thing they did in the morning was report to His Lordship. Reggie was thinking about reporting before breakfast but his daughters had beaten him to it. Her ladyship was obviously not happy and silently kissed her husband and left the bedroom. His Lordship said Reggie was now in charge of the estate, as he was no longer capable. He told Reggie the girls were running the estate and they would give him all the information he needed. His Lordship apologised and asked them to leave, as he was tired. Reggie looked at his father and said, "Now it is my time to be told how to run the estate." His father gave a weak smile and lay back on his bed.

Reggie took his daughters to the stables to look over the horses, his favourite animal. They both said they admired his horse. He was getting used to this talk in unison but it still threw him. He asked whether they rode horses and they told him his father had taught them to ride and they did not ride side-saddle; they had split skirts that allowed them to ride like men. Suddenly, they asked whether they might ride their father's horse. He told them, 'First things first' and that he was having trouble identifying Agnes from Elizabeth. They told him Agnes had a red ribbon in her hair and Elizabeth had a blue ribbon. After that introduction, Reggie looked towards his horse.

"This is a strong horse; he may not like you riding him."

"May we talk to him?"

"Yes, you certainly can talk to him."

Reggie leaned on the rails as the twins approached his horse. They spoke very quietly and then they separated and talked again. The horse was looking back and forward at each girl. The horse was listening to them but seemed confused about who was speaking. Reggie could not believe what he was seeing. Then they approached the horse and told him Agnes would ride him and then Elizabeth. They pointed to each other and identified themselves. This was a large horse and Elizabeth helped Agnes mount it. Reggie held his breath but Agnes said something in the horse's ear and they rode out of the stable. After a short time, they came back. Agnes dismounted and Elizabeth mounted and rode out of the stable. Reggie was so shocked that he could say nothing.

Later, Reggie went to his father to tell him the story. His mother entered the room and said, "You should not let those girls ride your horse."

"Mother, I think if my horse could answer you, he would tell us that he preferred my daughters riding him."

"They should be riding side-saddle."

"No, mother, I always thought riding side saddle was a crazy way to ride a horse. My daughters treat my horse like they have grown up together."

With that, his mother left the room, making an unintelligible remark.

His father was smiling.

"Well, father, I will see how well these girls ride; we will do a tour of the estate and the surrounding countryside."

"They will surprise you; they always surprise me."

Reggie went back to the stables to find his daughters grooming his horse.

"Get your horses saddled up and we will go for a ride around the estate and beyond."

As he mounted, the horse moved as though in protest. Reggie had watched the horse stand still when his daughters mounted, so he lent forward and whispered in the horse's ear, "I know you like my daughters better than me but I am your master." The horse's ears twitched and

Reggie smiled. Like his daughters, he talked to horses and had done so since he learned to ride.

As they rode around the farm, Reggie rode behind the girls and he held his breath as they jumped over a low fence. He caught up with the twins and said they should leave the estate. They rode along a road and headed for a small forest. He watched the girls handle the trees and then told them to head back to the estate. These girls were good riders and they had lived up to his expectations. When they reached the stables, he asked about the other horses. They told him they would buy unbroken horses and with the aid of the groom, would break them in. They would generally buy ponies but they also bought cart horses. Their method was to talk to the horses and gain their confidence. There had only been one failure and they thought the horse had mental problems. They sold him to the butcher for horse meat. Reggie told them to meet him in his father's study the next morning after breakfast.

Reggie went to his father to report and he praised him for teaching the girls to ride. His father told him they could shoot too and they shot a fox bothering the hens. They also shot rabbits on occasions when the cook wanted rabbit stew. Reggie had come home to two very capable daughters and wondered if any sons could be better.

The next day, they met in the office and the twins were there to tell him about the estate.

"Where do you sleep?"

"We sleep downstairs in the servant's quarters."

"Why don't you sleep upstairs?"

"We think it was suggested but her ladyship objected."

"That will have to change," Reggie muttered under his breath. The girls had excellent hearing and heard what he said but they kept silent.

"Now tell me about the cattle."

"We have extended the herd considerably; we have a local dairy that buys our milk. We keep a few cows for our consumption and to make butter, we sell some to a cheese maker and get cheese from him. The dairy sends a married couple to milk the cows allotted to them. We also have a bull."

"I did not see a bull yesterday."

"He is with a local farmer, siring some of his herd and we have a financial arrangement; you will see it in the accounts. We keep a separate account for the herd. We normally show our grandfather but lately he has been leaving it to us."

Reggie was taken aback by the girls talking about a bull siring cows.

"How do you know which cows to milk for estate consumption?"

"They have names and we call them to different stalls to be milked by us. Some cows go to Agnes and some to Elizabeth." This was all said in unison and Reggie was getting used to this dual speak.

"Let's go to the field; I have to see this."

They went to the field and the twins stood slightly apart. They called out Mary and then called Lizzie. Mary came and went to Agnes, who patted her on the head. Lizzie went to Elizabeth, who patted her on the head. Reggie was shaking his head; he had never seen anything like it before. He suggested they go back to the office and have morning tea; he actually thought he needed something stronger. Reggie said he had to visit Bertie and tomorrow they would discuss the rest of the estate. He asked what they would do the rest of the day.

"We will go to the garden plot after finding out what the cook needs. We will do a little weeding as well. We will probably peel potatoes for the cook and if she needs rabbits, we will go and shoot them.

"Tell the cook to wait for the rabbits till tomorrow; I want to see you shoot rabbits."

Reggie rode to Birmingham to meet Bertie; they went to the men's club for lunch.

"I have come home to a sick father, a mother living in the last century and twin daughters who are amazing to me with everything they do. I am getting used to their speaking in unison but when it comes to talking to cows, I think I am in another world."

"They talk to the horses and the chickens as well but they tell me the chickens are more difficult," Bertie said while laughing.

"We have not yet talked about the chickens. I am at a loss for what to do. I know I should take over but they are doing such a good job."

"Take over slowly and then we have to find them something to do. Go with them to the markets and you will see men fawning over them and they are treated with respect. I think the auctioneers and sellers are relieved when they are not there. They know you will take over and will not be a silent partner like our father. If they were men, I would send them out to manage other estates but that is not going to happen with girls. As for our mother, encourage her to go to Oxford as often as possible. Our father is the real problem. I talk to the doctor regularly and he is pessimistic. With all that information, let's have a brandy or whisky before lunch."

"Good idea. By the way, I notice you and Elsie have your meals separately."

"Yes, Elsie is scared of our mother and feels uncomfortable in her presence."

"That has to change; we are one family and I am going to give the girls a room upstairs and use my army training to get our mother in line."

"Best of luck with that but try not to let her upset our father."

"Yes, I think I have to bide my time; now let's have lunch and discuss finances."

After lunch, Bertie told Reggie that their father had an extensive portfolio of shares. He had invested wisely, mainly in banks and trading companies. The dividends alone could keep the estate running. He had land in Birmingham, with only a small portion developed for housing. Much of that land could be developed or sold for development; Birmingham was growing. Their mother had inherited land in Oxford and Bertie understood that it was returning an income. His mother had never told him this but the only relative in Oxford who communicated with him had told him some details. The twins had a trust fund, which Bertie managed. His Lordship had set it up just in case you disinherited them. This was set up before you came home, when they were ten.

"I think if they disinherited me, they would be the winners. This life is so different from the army and I will have a lot of adjusting to do. I have many social events to attend and I want to keep up with my army friends. The estate must come first."

The next day, Reggie met with the twins to discuss the rest of the farm. They told him egg production was bringing in a substantial income. The dairy would take most of the production the estate did not need. These girls were producing professionally kept accounts and that was one area that did not interest Reggie.

"Girls, I want you to carry on running this estate, but, of course, you have to report to me." He half expected them to say yes, sir.

"I have to circulate and meet people. I have been out of this social scene for a long time and I need to be seen. I have army friends to visit and financial contacts to make, so I may not be on the estate all the time."

"We understand and maybe you should look for a wife."

That surprised Reggie and under other circumstances, he would have told them to mind their own business but these were daughters looking for a mother.

"Well, no one has asked me."

"Ha! Ha! That was Uncle Bertie's reply when we asked him."

Reggie had a romantic liaison in South Africa but the lady did not want to come back to England with him, so that encounter ended. That lady would have been an ideal mother for his daughters; she rode and had a very strong character. He decided to ignore the twins' remark for the moment but it would remain in his thoughts.

Reggie decided to go to London for a few days and told the twins they were in charge. He gave no reason and now the twins were left guessing the reason. Bertie said his brother might have a pension or maybe he wanted to talk to the war office. That remark had the twins very impressed. Reggie had heard that two members of his brigade were in a military hospital in London. The twins talk about a wife was also on his mind. Getting away to London was a relief.

The girls carried on as normal and reported to His Lordship. He asked how they were getting along with their father; after all, he was used to giving orders and not taking them. They replied that they were telling him all about the estate and he had not given them any orders but had asked lots of questions. His Lordship was happy, as he knew Reggie would have to exert his authority in the near future. The bull was back on the estate and was in his own field; the girls talked to him but he was not as obedient as the cows.

Reggie wanted to visit the London Military Hospital but he also had to socialise and join a club so he could relax when he came to London. He went to the hospital to talk to the matron. He found her office and introduced himself, telling her he was retired from the army and really had no rank. She was a quiet older lady who asked what she could do for him. He told her he was here to visit veterans of the Boer War and he knew there were at least two officers in the hospital from his brigade. She told him there was a captain and a lieutenant but additionally, there was a sergeant. He thought for a moment and then asked her to take him to the sergeant. The man recognised Reggie right away and wanted to salute.

"Relax, soldier. I am no longer in the army and I want to know if you are being treated well."

The man said, "The hospital is doing its best but my problem is boredom. I come from Newcastle in the Northeast and so none of my relatives can visit me."

Reggie said, "I will see what I can do."

Reggie then went to see the lieutenant, who was in a ward with three other junior officers. The lieutenant explained that he was shot in the shoulder and was recuperating. His parents were coming from Devon soon to take him home. He was full of praise for the nursing staff.

The last call was on a captain who had been shot in the abdomen and the matron had said he had a long way to go but, so far, no infection. He had lost a lot of blood; however, blood transfusions appeared to be working.

Reggie entered a two-man ward and immediately recognised the captain from his battalion. There was another officer in the ward with a good-looking lady attending him. Reggie shook the captain's hand and said saluting was not necessary as he was no longer in the army. The captain introduced his ward partner, who was a major with a similar injury. The major introduced his widowed sister and all four started a discussion. The major had been in the infantry and so did not know Reggie but he had heard of a brigade roaming about the countryside. Reggie asked the lady about her husband. He had been killed at the siege of Ladysmith and now she wanted to get her brother home to Leicestershire. They had a long discussion until the matron came in to say visiting time was over. Reggie knew when he had been ordered to leave. He left with the lady, who was called Alice. She told Reggie she visited her brother as often as she could but the problem was leaving her ageing parents to look after a small estate. She said she was going back home but would visit her brother the following weekend.

    Reggie went to a club where he knew there would be army officers. He was allowed into the club on a temporary day membership and if he could find a proposer and seconder, he could join the club. As soon as he walked into the lounge, he saw five men he knew. He approached their table and they all stood and greeted him. Two of the older men he had known in South Africa before the war and one of the others, had been in his brigade. There was no problem gaining a proposer and seconder and he easily met the criteria to apply for membership. They chatted for an hour about the army and the war, then apologised as they had to leave to go to a function. They told him that the club had a restaurant where he could get dinner and they hoped they would see him in the future. He said that he would come back to London the following weekend.

Reggie sat in a very comfortable armchair with his whisky and thought about the sergeant and the lady, Alice. He would leave for Birmingham on the train the following morning and investigate the trains to Newcastle. He was determined that the sergeant would be reunited with his family. At dinner, the waiter told him if he did not finish his wine, they would put his name on the bottle and he could retrieve it the next time he came to the club. He found himself thinking about retrieving Alice.

From the train to Birmingham, he went straight to Bertie's office to find his daughters visiting their uncle. They asked about his trip to London and he said he had visited some wounded soldiers from his regiment. They all went to lunch and Reggie was in a good mood. Afterwards, they retired back to Bertie's office and because the twins were sitting behind their father; he forgot they were there and started telling Bertie about the sergeant. The twins already knew a sergeant was well below a brigadier. Reggie was telling Bertie he had to get this man to Newcastle when he realised the twins were sitting behind him. They were almost in tears.

"I am sorry, that was not for your ears."

"Father, we want to be nurses and what you have just said reinforced our desire."

"Bertie, I am blessed with two daughters who surpass my expectations and I declare that they will surely make the best nurses in England."

The twins were blushing as well as trying to stop their tears. Bertie said they had already completed a preliminary course in nursing and he was about to enrol them in the second course.

"Do you have any whisky? I want to toast that development."

"I only have brandy but I am sure that will do."

The twins watched as their father and uncle toasted them. They travelled back to the estate and Reggie told the girls that the next morning they would discuss their future. In private, the twins discussed what people would think about their plans and decided that, with the exception of their grandmother, they would all be very supportive. The next morning, Reggie told his daughters he would hire a new milk maid and they would train her to take over their duties so that they would then enrol in the second nurse's course. He would investigate which hospitals had war veterans and get them some part-time work. If they needed any other help, they should let him know, as he would be going to London regularly. They told him everything would run smoothly and he should not worry, enjoy London and give their best wishes to the sergeant. That remark made him smile, as the sergeant was only part of his thoughts.

The new milk maid was a young girl and she was provided with a room in the servant's quarters. She had left school at thirteen and worked on her father's small farm, eight miles away. She was familiar with milking but was fascinated when the twins had to introduce her to the cows, calling each cow by name. She had been wide-eyed when the twins talked to her in unison but this was something new again. They called a cow, introduced the milk maid and allowed her to milk the cow. The twin then embraced the cow. They then called another cow with the same procedure. Each time, they hugged both the maid and the cow after milking. On the following day, they asked her to call the cows and then milk them. It worked well and on the third day they stood outside the sight of the cows; everything went perfectly. Now they were relieved of milking.

 Reggie was visiting several Birmingham hospitals to find war veterans. There was no designated military hospital as such, so these soldiers were scattered about in normal hospitals. He decided there was one hospital with the most veterans and he approached the matron there to see if the hospital would take on his daughter's part time. She told him she would have to interview them first but was willing to take them on as nurse's assistants.

The twins presented themselves at the matron's office and said their names. The matron sat quite still for several seconds, staring at the girls, before she told them to introduce themselves again. Reggie had not forewarned the matron about his daughter's manner of speech, having become quite accustomed to it.

"Do you always speak like that?"

"Yes, matron, we are identical twins; we talk together and think together."

"Well, I can't tell you apart, so I have a small medal here that Agnes could pin to her apron and then I, along with everyone else, will have a chance of telling who is who. Well, I think that you two might brighten up things in some of our wards. I understand you have completed an introductory nursing course and are taking a second course at the Institute."

"Yes, matron, we are practicing bandaging and we think we have mastered the technique."

"The bandaging may be easy but it is what is under the bandages that might be more difficult."

"We have delivered calves and foals and have helped a midwife."

"Well, I will take you to the ward with the wounded soldiers; it can be a glum place as some of the men feel abandoned and that they may never leave the hospital. I will let you walk in first and I will linger behind. I hope you are not offended by bad words, as some of the language can be very foul."

"We think we will cope," they said in unison.

As they entered the ward, a man in a wheelchair said, "Look, lads, two beauties."

"Thank you, sir. I am Agnes (pointing to herself and Elizabeth pointing at her) and I am Elizabeth (same routine)."

The man sat open-mouthed and several of the other patients sat up to pay attention to this new development. There was silence for a few seconds and finally the man asked whether they could do that again.

"Yes, we always speak this way and we think alike, even if we are separated."

"I have to see this."

Now all the men were attentive, even the ones who could not sit up.

"We will demonstrate for you; Agnes will stay in the ward and allow a man to ask a question. Elizabeth will take the soldier in the wheelchair into another ward. She will tell him the answer but he will not know the question."

Now even the matron was intrigued and reflected that the twins had already brightened up the ward. She had been sitting by the door and had not said a word.

After Elizabeth had left the ward with the soldier in the wheelchair, one man asked whether Agnes's father had been in the army and if so, what was his rank? Agnes answered that her father was a brigadier (which resulted in a murmur in the ward). Elizabeth came back and the soldier was asked the answer; his answer "brigadier," brought a round of applause. Now the twins went to each patient and asked about his ailment; the whole ward was a buzz. As they were leaving, one man shouted, "Will you marry me?"

"Do you have a twin? If the answer is no, we cannot marry you."

Now the whole room erupted in laughter.

"Well, that went very well," said the matron. "We can't normally get a smile from those men. I think you might cheer up the whole hospital."

Reggie was waiting in the matron's office to take them home.

"Sir, you did not tell me about your daughters. They have just had a whole room of wounded soldiers laughing and that is a miracle."

Reggie could not help but smile; he knew how a ward of wounded soldiers could be a miserable place. They rode back to the estate together and their father said he was going to give them a room upstairs in the manor but was waiting till his father's health improved. He wanted the whole family to eat meals together but because of his mother, that may take some time to achieve. The twins talked about the soldiers and Reggie asked if they had used bad language. They told him there were some swear words from the men when they were describing their pain or injuries but the twins were not offended. They said the soldiers were actually very polite. This surprised Reggie enormously, as he was thinking the only polite soldiers, he knew were the junior officers who knew his rank. Some of the most impolite soldiers were the generals.

At the weekend, Reggie went back to London and inquired about the process for sending the sergeant to Newcastle. He could get a bed, put in a luggage waggon and the military ambulance could take the sergeant to the train station. The matron had a nurse on staff who came from the north-east and she would travel with the sergeant. Reggie would pay for everything, including a return ticket for the nurse. The sergeant was very happy with the proposal as he was going back to his hometown. His gratitude to Reggie was heartfelt and genuine; he said he had never known such kindness from an officer. The nurse was also happy to be able to visit family and friends at no cost in time or money.

Reggie took Alice to dinner after a little hesitation on her part. He described his daughters to her and was pleased that she was not upset by the revelation; in fact, she was interested in seeing them. Reggie said it was a long ride from the manor but he would bring his daughters to see Alice. She said they could stay in her house overnight, as she spent most of her time with her parents on the estate. Everything was going very well except for his father's health. The twins were very popular in the hospital; there were four officers in one ward who treated everyone with rudeness and disdain. Agnes and Elizabeth completely won these men over on their very first encounter; after that, they complained that the twins did not visit them often enough!

The twins also cheered up the patients in other civilian wards and along the way, met many men who had been injured at work. The matron gave them permission to go anywhere in the hospital and to maybe try to cheer up the nurses and doctors as well as the patients. A senior surgeon came to ask the matron about these two nurses, as they had stunned him.

Reggie was considering a future life with Alice and told the twins they would be going for a long ride and asked, "Did they think they were up for it?" Their reply was that they could be in the saddle for hours if they could rest the horses occasionally. Reggie found the village on the map and told them about Alice. He said he wanted to marry her if she would have him but they were definitely not about to tell Alice the information. The twins were delighted and dying to meet this lady.

The ride was indeed a long one and when they were nearing the village, they stopped for a drink at a pub. As they entered the bar, it went very quiet and Reggie asked what his daughters wanted to drink. They replied together that they would like a ginger beer and the barman stiffened in surprise. Reggie ordered a pint of local beer and two ginger beers but the barman still stood motionless. Reggie told him these girls often had the same effect on many people when they first met. Finally, they received their drinks and Reggie decided that they would sit outside in order to allow the bar to operate normally. However, he had to admit to himself that he loved the reaction his twins produced to unknown people.

They obtained directions to the estate, which was only a few miles away. As they arrived at the estate, Alice was sitting outside in the sun with her parents. They dismounted and Reggie introduced Alice to his daughters. Even though she had been forewarned, Alice was still surprised when the girls spoke. Her parents had not been warned and they were in shock. Alice showed them around the estate, which had stables, a milk shed and four fields. There were a few dairy cattle and a small herd of beef cattle. They did have a pigsty with four pigs. The girls were asking themselves why they had no pigs.

The staff was one farmhand, a cook and a milkmaid. Alice's mother used to milk the cows but as she got older, her hands become stiff. The father tended to the horses but mucking out the stable was becoming too much for him. They were looking forward to their son coming home from the hospital but knew he would be of little help on the estate. Alice said she did not ride very much but she would use her small carriage to take them to her house. They could settle in and then come back for dinner. The girls offered to help the cook but Alice said that was not necessary.

The house was the largest in the village and had five bedrooms. Alice explained that it belonged to her in-laws but they had died not long after learning of the death of their son. She said they died of grief. The house was legally hers but she rarely used it and had a cleaner come in once a week. There was a place for the horses but it was only a covered shed. Alice left and Reggie explored the house, as he was particularly interested in the library, which was quite extensive. The girls went to look at the garden, which was overgrown and then went to tidy the kitchen and wash some pots and pans. They were not sure what to do next but were unsure whether to ask their father, as this was all a new experience for them.

They rode to the estate later and had dinner. The girls spent the most time talking to Alice's parents. They had offered to serve the food but once she had adjusted to their speech, the cook refused to let them. Alice was impressed with the girls and her father agreed; he said these two ladies could have no equal. Reggie always thought of them as girls but in reality, at twenty-three, they were ladies. On the ride home the next day, the twins were telling their father they wanted to return in order to fix the stables and the garden plots at the house and on the estate. They also asked their father whether they could have pigs; that made him laugh.

They arrived at their own estate to find His Lordship very sick and fading fast. Reggie and the twins entered His Lordship's bedroom to find Bertie and her ladyship already there. When her ladyship saw the twins, she frowned and Reggie, in turn gave her a stern look. His Lordship rallied a little when the twins gave him a kiss, then they went to the back of the room. Reggie had seen men die before but this was different. As they watched, His Lordship closed his eyes and stopped breathing; everyone in the room was motionless and the twins started to weep. Bertie whispered to Reggie that he thought his father had hung on to have his last sight of the twins. Reggie went to the study and put his head in his hands. The girls went to their room and could not stop crying; her ladyship, however, did not shed a tear.

The next few days on the estate were very quiet, with Reggie staying in the office, the twins staying in their rooms and her ladyship staying in her room. Bertie was the only one planning for the future. He sought out Reggie and said after the funeral they had a big problem; it was called the estate tax, often known as death duty. He explained the tax to Reggie and said they may be able to retain the estate but have to sell some assets. Reggie was in no mood to understand the tax; he had to plan the funeral.

Bertie decided to talk to the twins about the pending problem and they rewarded his faith in them by coming up with some good ideas. Maybe they could sell most of the herd to the dairy and let the herd stay on the estate. There were several horses that they could sell to raise money and most of the egg production could be sold to the dairy. Bertie understood Reggie's problem but the twins seemed to have a better understanding of the situation. Bertie had never dealt with the estate tax and would have to find out the details. The assessment and payment processes had to be understood. He also had to find out if there was a grace period for payment and if it could be paid in instalments.

Reggie sent word to Alice's brother that he would not be in London for a few weeks due to the death of his father. He was already missing the comfort of Alice's company. Finally, Bertie got Reggie's attention about their ideas and he took the twins with him to help find solutions to the financial problems looming. The land held in Birmingham could be sold for development to build houses, as there was a strong demand for houses near the city centre and industry. He did not want to sell any shares if he could help it, as the dividends were good and produced an ongoing income. He had approached the dairy and they would buy the herd. Their father had a very good bank account; he had been very frugal. The horses could be sold and in particular, Reggie's horse would bring a good price. Even the twins rejected that proposal but Reggie agreed to the sale because he did not want to sell any estate land. The twins said they had money in the bank but Reggie said he would not touch their money.

The funeral was planned and everyone was in black. Relatives came from Oxford and were accommodated on the estate. The twins were very discreet but their father told them they were his father's favourites and he would not see them pushed into the background. Reggie was telling his relatives from Oxford about the twins, much to the annoyance of his mother. The twins had already bewitched their relatives when they spoke together.

Reggie had decided they would have a wake and had employed a man to play the bagpipes and a band to play some military music. He was not keen on letting people dance but was happy that they should just sit and enjoy the music. He would have liked to invite Alice but there was no time and it was hard to get her to the estate. The twins agreed that the funeral and the wake were a fitting tribute to their grandfather. They were planning on devoting all their energies to Alice's stables and the gardens. They went to the farmer's market to look at pigs; that could be their next challenge. One of the auctioneers asked why they were not bidding. And they told him about their grandfather's death. The matron was informed they would take some time off and she understood. When they finally returned to the hospital, they were greeted by cheering and clapping.

Reggie had a problem; he wanted to ask Alice to marry him but he had to settle the estate tax. He decided he would take a carriage to Leicestershire with the twins; he would leave them there and bring Alice back to his estate. The twins were very happy with this arrangement, as they could help Alice's parents put their estate in order and at the same time, they were also interested in how to treat and maintain pigs. When the day came to travel, Reggie drove the twins, with them sitting in the back of the carriage like ladies of leisure. He had not driven a carriage before and they had a few near misses with carts but he started to learn not to cut in too fast after overtaking. The twins were having great fun in the back, enjoying the scenery. Reggie had brought a hamper with food and they had a picnic by the side of the road. Late in the afternoon, they reached Alice's estate; the twins could see by Alice's face that they were very welcome, particularly Reggie.

Alice's parents were also there to welcome them and the twins asked Alice's father what they could do.

"Rest for tonight; that was a long journey and you must be tired."

"We only sat in the back of the carriage while our father did all the work."

These two, speaking in unison, still threw the old man.

"Well, have a walk around and see what needs attention."

The twins headed for the stables to greet the horses. There were five horses, one of which was a carthorse and the others were riding horses. There was a large thoroughbred that must be Alice's brother's horse and they went to talk to him. The old man followed the twins to the stables and watched as they were talking to the horses. He wondered whether the horses were as confused by the ladies as he was.

Reggie and the twins went to Alice's house and deposited their luggage. Alice and her parents followed in Alice's carriage. Her father suggested that this was a small village and that they would like to visit the pub for refreshments. He wanted to see how the villagers would react to the twins. Reggie was all for a drink and so they all walked to the pub. Alice's mother was a bit reluctant to go inside but her husband said it could be entertaining. This was a one-room pub and there were women in the bar. They entered the bar and it went quiet. Alice's father told them to carry on as he was entertaining guests. The conversations resumed until the twins were asked what they would like to drink. They said, "Ginger beer, please." All conversation stopped and the barman stood stock still.

"Come on, Fred, the ladies want a drink."

The bar was completely silent and so the twins said, "Don't worry, we always talk like this."

Reggie, Alice and Alice's mother were all laughing. Alice's father suggested they sit outside to get the benefit of the summer evening's fading sunlight. As they left the bar, they heard the conversation start and knew it was all about the twins. Reggie was talking to Alice's parents about the death duty, as it was weighing heavily on his mind. Alice's father said that when his father died not long ago, as he lived to a great age, they had to sell a lot of property, most of it in and around the village. His father used to own the pub. Reggie said that he was hoping he could retain most of his estate.

Early the next day, Reggie and Alice left for Birmingham and the twins were left on the estate. They immediately gravitated to the stables, where they exercised the horses and then started cleaning the stables (mucking out). Alice's father was watching and said to his wife, "These young ladies look and think alike and they work so well together that I doubt whether two lads would do better. They talk to the horses and the cattle and I think they have tried the pigs. Get some refreshments prepared; I will go and tell them to have a rest."

As he approached the twins, they were near the henhouse. There was a fence and the twins were examining part of the fence.

"We think either a fox or dog has been digging under the fence to try to get at the hens. He may have been disturbed, as we were here early this morning. We are sure he will be back. May we sleep on the estate tonight and do you have a couple of rifles?"

"You certainly can sleep here. I was wondering and a bit worried about two ladies alone in Alice's house. I have rifles and shotguns; take your pick."

"We don't like shotguns, as the pellets tend to spray out. Rifles are better if we get a good shot and we think we will."

"Well, we should retire for refreshments; you must be tired."

"We are thirsty but not tired; we need to take a look at the cattle."

They retired to the house and looked over the rifles. They then rode over to Alice's house and brought some of their clothes back to the estate. They said they would go back the next day to tend to the garden and the following day to tend to the estate garden.

In front of the cook, Alice's father said to his wife, "These girls never stop; they make me feel tired." They all laughed.

Reggie reached the estate to find Bertie in the office. Alice was introduced and Reggie said Alice should stay with the men as they talked about the estate. He knew that he wanted her to be his wife and felt she should have nothing hidden from her. Bertie told them the estate was being valued by a very professional value company. He had told them not to underestimate the value, as he did not want a problem with the taxation people. Many estates were being crippled by this tax but there was no way of evading it. The estate was one of the smaller ones and he thought that they might have to pay seven or 7.5 per cent tax on the value.

    Reggie said they should take refreshments and that he wanted to introduce Alice to his mother, Elsie and Benjamin. Alice met her ladyship and the welcome was a bit subdued but not cold or unpleasant. Her ladyship did mention that Leicestershire was not quite Oxfordshire. Reggie bristled at this implied insult and Bertie gave him a look to say, 'Let it go'. Elsie and Benjamin were most welcoming and Alice mentioned to Reggie that she missed having children. That had Reggie thinking but first things first, he had to get rid of this estate tax.

    In the afternoon, the three assembled again in the office. Bertie told them that the will was under probate but he knew the details and things were not looking too bad. Their father had been very good with money and investments. In the past five years, his worth has grown through the purchase of additional stocks and shares. The bank balance had been growing as the stocks had been giving good dividends. Their father had realised that after his death, the estate duty could be large. Accordingly, he had given two fields of the estate and some shares to Bertie and they could not be counted on the estate. Bertie recognised that Reggie would inherit the estate and he had no use for those two fields. His lordship had also left a significant amount in his will for the twins. He had set up a trust for them and continually put money into their account. Alice asked about the twins.

Bertie looked at Reggie, who said Alice knew the twins had been born out of wedlock but did not yet know that they were his.

Bertie took up the tale, saying, "Just after the twins were born, our father thought they must be his grandchildren but he had no way to prove it. He made himself guardian and when our mother asked, he told her they were born on the estate, so he had to be their guardian. He could not acknowledge them as his granddaughters until Reggie came home when they were ten. He decided that the family would keep quiet so as not to destroy Reggie's career."

Reggie wanted Alice to know everything.

"He taught them to ride, to shoot and to fish; he watched them talk to the animals. He taught them to keep the accounts and he basically let them run the estate from about the age of fifteen. When we discussed the twins at a later time, he told me he wished he had not kept their relationship secret. He said he had made the decision and generally, our father was not a man to change his decisions. Although I think when the twins twisted his arm, he may have gone back on some decisions. They made the deal with the dairy to milk most of the cows. They also made the deal with the cheese maker and all our father did was approve their decisions. He told me one of his delights in life was going to the farmer's markets with the twins. Firstly, there was the shock value when they spoke to strangers. Then, on top of that, they were excellent negotiators, whether buying or selling; all he had to do was pay or receive money. They also knew their cattle and particularly horses; they were always buying and selling horses."

Reggie was regretting not having that experience.

"Our mother never acknowledged the twins and I think that caused a rift in their relationship. Our father always seemed to be happier when our mother was away. He wanted them to move upstairs but they told him they were comfortable in the servant's quarters. Finally, when he was dying, I think he hung on till Reggie and the twins returned from Leicestershire. He wanted to see them for the last time. Sorry, Reggie, I think he was mainly waiting for the twins."

Reggie breathed deeply through his nose and said, "I need a drink."

Alice thanked Bertie for his frankness and said that she knew the twins were special. They retired to the lounge, where Alice was introduced to two of her ladyship's friends. Reggie was wondering whether they knew about the twins but he was not going to spoil their afternoon tea.

Meanwhile, in Leicestershire, the twins had tried the two rifles and shot a couple of pigeons. The cook said she would cook pigeon pie if they could kill a couple more pigeons, so, of course, they went out and shot more pigeons. At dinner, Alice's father was telling them some family history. They had three children: the first was a son, who was the major in the hospital; the second was Alice; and the third was a boy who died at birth. The twins said they had helped a midwife and they had seen a stillbirth. They then looked at Alice's mother and apologised. She was close to tears but said, "Do not take any notice of me; I have two fine children."

Then they told Alice's parents about their hospital work. There was lots of laughter and the mother said it was a pity they were not in the London hospital, as their son said he was bored. The twins said they would love to meet him, as they could tell him how much they loved his horse. After dinner, the twins excused themselves, as they wanted to get up before dawn in the hope of shooting a fox. When they had left the dining room, Alice's father told his wife that he had watched them shoot pigeons with ease and thought his son was not as good a shot.

Before dawn, the twins awoke to hear the hens making a noise and they instinctively knew that the fox was trying to get into the henhouse. They looked out of the window to see a shape near the fence. They loaded the rifles and in their nightdresses, they exited from the kitchen. They took aim at the fox and two shots simultaneously disturbed the morning peace. The light was just dawning but two bullets hit the fox, one in the head and the other in the chest. They walked over to the fox and decided they had to bury it, as it was obviously dead. Agnes went to the stables to get spades while Elizabeth watched the dead fox just in case it moved.

Alice's father was a light sleeper and had been woken by two gunshots. He went to the window to watch two young ladies drag a dead fox to a grave they had dug. He dressed quickly and was on his way to the twins, saying to himself that he wanted these young ladies to be his granddaughters. They showed him the carcass and pointed to the bullet holes. All he could say was, "well done." He was lost for words. Breakfast was taken early as the twins wanted to get to Alice's house to put her garden in order.

Back on the estate, Reggie proposed marriage and Alice said yes but to wait until her brother was home. Reggie had a new mission: to get her brother out of the hospital as soon as possible. First, he had to get Alice home and pick up the twins. The estate tax was temporarily out of his mind as Bertie told him this would take time and there was plenty of time to do other things. Alice had been busy; she talked to Reggie's mother in private and also to Elsie. She thought she could handle the mother, who she recognised had very set ideas. Elsie was a delight and Alice decided she would make a good sister-in-law. She loved Benjamin, who entertained her and had her thinking about having children. Reggie was not thinking about more children but that was a problem for another time.

Reggie and Alice arrived at her estate to be greeted by Alice's very happy parents. Her father was unhappy the twins would be leaving; he was telling his daughter she should visit her house to see her transformed garden. Reggie said they would stay overnight and leave early in the morning. He was anxious to talk to Bertie but loath to leave Alice.

The dinner was entertaining and after dinner, Reggie and the twins departed for Alice's house. Alice was then asked by her father whether she would marry Reggie.

"Most certainly," was her reply. Her father said that this was a splendid development.

"I think you have changed, father; I don't think you really approved of my first marriage, as it was a love marriage, not an arranged marriage."

"No, I think you could have done better but this is different this time. I want granddaughters and these two ladies are my choice."

"I suspected these two young ladies had charmed you; I will be marrying their father and I have said yes."

Her mother came and kissed her, with tears in her eyes; her father was toasting her with wine.

"Before anything happens, my brother must come home from London and Reggie is going to arrange that."

This was a happy estate.

Reggie and the twins arrived home to be greeted by Bertie. He was glad to see them, as he had organised a deal to sell the Birmingham land to be developed into housing. The sale of that land would cover a large portion of the estate tax. He had also arranged to sell the herd to the dairy and the cattle would remain on the estate. The dairy would also take care of egg production. They might have to sell some of the horses and the tax would be covered. Reggie was happy but all he could think of was the immediate problem of getting Alice's brother back to his home.

The twins went to their room to discuss the developments. They were happy with the cattle sale and knew nothing about the Birmingham land but they did not want to sell the horses. They suspected their father would sell his horse. The twins set their sights ongoing to London to help Alice's brother. The big surprise was when their father visited them and said they should move to a room upstairs. They should also sit beside him at dinner and be a couple of minutes earlier so he can make the seating arrangements. He asked Bertie to also bring Elsie and Benjamin to dinner.

Reggie arranged so the twins would sit either side of him and Bertie would sit with his wife and son at the other end of the table. His mother could sit where she wished. They were all present when her ladyship entered. She looked around at the table and said, "Where do I sit? I should be next to you, Reggie."

"Mother, first of all, meals will be a family affair. Until I have a wife, my daughters will sit on either side of me. When I have a wife, she will decide which side she wants to sit on and the twins will sit on the other side. Mother, you can sit where you wish and a place setting will be made for you."

Reggie was breaking all the traditional rules. Her ladyship snorted and was about to leave.

"Mother, if you leave, you will get no dinner; I will not allow food to be sent to your room."

Everyone was silent, even Benjamin. Her ladyship sat down near Bertie and a place setting was made for her.

This was a quiet meal until, near the end, the twins could not resist asking about selling horses.

"We will all go to the stables and sort out the horses to sell; my horse should fetch a good price."

"May we go to the market and buy two unbroken horses? We have our own money."

"You may buy them but I will pay; we don't have to pay this dreaded tax yet and if you can break them in, we might sell them."

Her ladyship was watching this conversation and in her mind, she thought the twins were too forward. Bertie, however, was enjoying this conversation.

"Sorry to interrupt, Father; we have a request. May we go to London to escort Alice's brother safely to Leicester?"

"You must be reading my mind; I will be going to London this weekend to make travel arrangements. When all that is in place, I will take you to London to see the sights and take the major home."

The twins were delighted and Bertie said he would also take Elsie to London to see the sights. All except her ladyship were in an excited mood; she could not wait to get to Oxford to escape what she saw as a definite turn for the worse in developments here. What her sons did not know was that she had sold some land and bought a house. She had hired a maid and a cook and had a part-time gardener. Bertie's cousin contact had gone to India and was part of the British Administration, so he was getting no information from Oxford and anyway, he was busy with the estate tax. Her ladyship left the next day for Oxford without telling Reggie; she told her maid to look for another job as she would not be back.

Reggie was angry when he found his mother gone but he had to exert his authority. Bertie was not very surprised, only that she left so abruptly without an argument. The twins told their father they hoped they were not the cause of their grandmother's departure. Reggie said there was no problem; they could now concentrate on getting the major home and then the wedding.

After the twins had left, Bertie wondered whether their mother would even come to the wedding. Reggie said that when they had a date, he would send her an explicit direction to attend the wedding; he was going to invite his uncles, the brothers of their mother, so she should be there.

Reggie went to London to meet Alice and talk to the major about the journey. He found that there had been one or two new casualties in the hospital as some Boers were still resisting the British army. There was a corporal from his old brigade who came from Bromyard. The man had lost a leg and Reggie saw that as a new task to get him home. Alice was in a very happy mood; she had never seen her parents so happy and most of it had to do with the twins. Of course, they were looking forward to their son coming home but they were ever so happy that the twins would bring him.

The twins had purchased a couple of unbroken horses at the market. These horses were not too highly strung, rather just not used to humans controlling them. The twins set about talking to the horses, for they knew that they would be gone from the estate at the end of the week and maybe away for up to a month. They spent several hours a day with the horses until, finally; they were taking food from their hands. The groom congratulated the girls on their achievement and said he would not try to ride the horses until they returned. The girls liked the groom and told him they were going to London. The furthest he had been to Worcester for the races.

Reggie was pleased about the report of two more horses potentially for sale. He was telling the twins to relax, although that was the last thing he could do. They were excited about the train to London and that they were going to stay in a hotel. This was a first and they were not sure what to expect. The station was huge and from the station they took a horse-drawn carriage that Reggie told them was called a Hackney carriage or cab. This city was much more crowded than Birmingham and there were people everywhere. Reggie looked amused at what the twins were saying and pointing at. They first went to the hotel to book in and leave their luggage. Reggie and the twins approached the desk; Reggie made the booking. The clerk looked funnily at the twins, so they said, "It is all right; we are his daughters."

Reggie wanted to laugh but the man was dumb struck. The manager came over and asked if there was a problem; the twins told him, "No problem" and now he too was speechless. It took a couple of minutes before the hotel came back to normal. The porter had watched all this in silence but he was smart enough to welcome the twins politely, earning himself a tip from Reggie. The twins had a single room with their own toilet and bath; they did not have that at home. Reggie told them that Alice stayed in this hotel and that they would come back after visiting the hospital. Now they were keen to leave the hotel.

They entered the hospital with almost everyone staring. As they entered the major's ward, they saw Alice sitting by a bed. The captain in the next bed could only stare open-mouthed. Alice's brother had been warned about the twins but when they spoke, he was still shocked. The twins kissed Alice and asked if they could kiss her brother. Her reply was that if she said no, she would lose a brother. The major was trying to think of something to say when the twins kissed him on each cheek. Alice told the twins to give the captain a kiss, so he did not feel left out. Neither the major nor the captain could speak before being kissed. Reggie watched his daughters do more than any enemy could – keep officers silent.

Finally, Alice told her brother that she would marry Reggie and that the twins would be his nieces. Then the major found his voice and said, "That means I can't marry them."

Alice replied, "No, you are too old anyway."

There was laughter when the captain said he was young enough and not related. The twins turned to him and asked if he was a twin. He replied that he had no twin and they then told him they could not marry a man without a twin. The room was now filled with laughter. A nurse came in to see if there was a problem. The twins told her together that there was no problem. The nurse stood for a second and then fled.

After a short time, Reggie said he had to visit a corporal from his brigade. The twins wanted to join him but he told them a ward full of ordinary soldiers could be a difficult place for young women like them. They reminded him that they regularly visited ordinary soldiers in the hospital in Birmingham. As they were leaving to visit the soldiers, Reggie said they would discuss the transport of Alice's brother when they came back.

The three entered the ward with the ordinary soldiers and the room immediately fell silent. They walked over to the corporal and Reggie introduced his daughters. The sight of them was enough for him to lose words but when they started greeting him, he was truly speechless. They shook his hand and suddenly he regained speech.

"Young ladies, I am sorry. I cannot bow to you and that is what I want to do."

"We understand you are from a farm in Bromyard; does your father have cattle?"

"Yes, my father has cattle and an orchard where we grow apples and pears. My father makes cider and I miss it so much."

"We will make sure our father gets you home so you can drink that cider."

Reggie was standing back and watching a soldier with tears running down his cheeks. The ward now had a buzz and a soldier shouted, "You lucky man." The twins turned towards the speaker and together they said all the soldiers were lucky to be back in England. The ward went silent at that but when they left, most patients were clapping and laughing. Reggie was telling Alice what had happened while the twins were entertaining her brother. They told him they loved his parents and now there were tears in his eyes. While they had been gone, Alice had told her brother that their father was really set on having the twins as granddaughters.

At dinner that evening, Reggie told them about the procedure on Monday. A military ambulance would pick up the major and the twins and take them to the train. They would be lodged in the luggage carriage and the major would be on his hospital bed. Reggie and Alice would be on the same train. At Leicester, they would be picked up by a military ambulance and Reggie would hire a carriage for Alice and himself. If the twins thought there was a problem, they could try to find the guard or pull the emergency cord but not do that unless there was a real emergency.

On Sunday, Reggie hired a Hackney carriage and took the twins on a sight-seeing tour. They saw the trooping of the colours and were admiring the horses. They saw Buckingham Palace and were admiring the guards. The Parliament at Westminster was impressive but the most fascinating sight of all to them was Tower Bridge. When the road opened to let a ship through, they were squealing with delight. Later, they were telling the captain and the major about this marvel. Neither of them had ever seen Tower Bridge.

Monday morning came and the twins and the major were all nervous. He told them he was nervous to get home to see his parents; they were nervous about the journey. The ambulance arrived and the men put the major on a stretcher and then onto a trolley. The twins stood back and did not speak, not wanting to upset the process. At the station, the trolley was taken to the luggage car and the men lifted the major onto the stretcher and put him on a special bed. Reggie had hired a medical bed, like they had in the hospital. There were two chairs for the twins and the guard opened a small window for light. He explained that when he shut the luggage car door, it would be quite dark. The twins nodded and one said that it was all right; they did not want to speak in unison to cause any delay.

The train started and there was some initial shaking but then it became smooth as the train got into rhythm with the clickety-clack of the wheels on the rails. The twins asked if they should talk, as this journey might take a few hours. The major said, "Please, tell me about your estate and my father's estate."

"We will start with your estate. First of all, we love your parents; they are so kind."

The major was starting to feel emotional. They described the house and the stables as their favourite places. The major closed his eyes and imagined what they were telling him. He had already been told how the twins talked to the animals but to hear it from them, it seemed so normal. They told him the pigs were the most difficult and it took quite a time to get them to come when called. He could remember those two big, fat pigs and could not imagine them ever coming when called.

The journey passed very quickly and when the carriage door was opened, they all had to blink at the brightness. Waiting on the platform were Reggie and Alice, full of smiles. The ambulance men took the major and the twins said they would ride in the ambulance, even though it was not too comfortable. Arriving at the estate, Alice's parents were waiting in an excited mood. The twins had suggested to them that, as they had a downstairs living room with double doors, they should put their son in that room. If he had a bed on wheels, the major could be taken out to the verandah when the weather was good. The major was inundated with kisses and hugs from his mother. He told her he wanted to get some air. Then his mother saw the twins and kissed them. Alice, the daughter of the house, had not yet had a welcome but found that she did not mind.

The welcome settled down and the father asked what the major would like. His request was a bit strange and surprising: he wanted to see his horse and the pigs. Everyone except the twins was bemused by the request. They went to the stables, brought the horse out and asked their father to hold him. They then went to the sty and called the pigs, who followed them around to the front of the house.

The major said, "Now that I have seen everything, there are no miracles left."

No one knew what he meant except the twins.

Reggie, Alice and the twins went to Alice's house to change clothes for the evening dinner. The major was left with his parents. He told them a little about the war but all he wanted to talk about was the twins and their effect on him. They had treated him so well and considerately; they had even apologised for riding his horse without his permission. Through their stories, they had told him enough, so he had good mental images of everything that they had been doing. He said that when they told him about the pigs, he could not believe those old pigs would obey anyone; that was why he called it a miracle. His parents were smiling the whole time he was talking. He wished he was fifteen years younger and had not been to war.

Reggie told the twins that he and Alice would leave the next day and asked if they would stay on for a few weeks. They replied that they would nurse Alice's brother and find a nurse for him. Reggie asked whether they could cope with an injured man.

"Father, we have nursed men with similar injuries. We know the problems of a man who cannot get out of bed. The only difference this time is that we are personally involved."

Reggie was having vivid visions of a bed-bound soldier.

"We hope that before we leave, we can have him in a wheelchair."

"I pray you succeed," said Alice.

The evening dinner was an entertaining affair, held around the major's bed. The twins had told his mother about a party where guests picked up their food from a central table and sat where they wanted, with their food on their laps. Everyone was surprised at how well it worked. Alice's father said this was the first time he had had a meal while not sitting at a table and they would surely do it again. The major had a whisky and some wine to toast his arrival home; these were his first drinks for a long while, as the nurses had been very strict in the hospital, not allowing any alcohol. The twins drank ginger beer; a case had been sent from the village pub.

Reggie and Alice went back to Birmingham to plan the wedding. They decided to have the church wedding in Leicestershire so that the major could attend. They were hoping that by the time of the wedding, he would be in a wheelchair. There would be a small reception and then a larger reception at the estate in Birmingham. They would send invitations to Reggie's mother and two of his uncle's families. Reggie was hoping his mother would come, as he had now found out she was living in her own house in Oxford; he thought that she may be more content now. Bertie had good news, telling them that the Death Duties had been finalised and the debt was covered by selling the Birmingham land, the dairy herd and four horses, not including Reggie's horse. That news deserved a celebration.

Back in Leicestershire, the major's health was improving with the help of the twins. He was still in pain but now able to sit up and he thought the fresh air was doing him good. The twins would ride the horses close to his window so he could see them; that cheered him up to no end. They would make him laugh by also taking the cows and pigs for a walk past his window. His parents watched on with great delight and saw the steady improvement in their son. They could never imagine it happening without the positive influence of the twins. They knew their son would never walk again but held new hope that he would at least be mobile in a wheelchair, not confined to a bed for the rest of his life.

Meanwhile, Reggie had arranged to transport the corporal to Birmingham to be housed for a few days before going to Bromyard. The twins were going to London to pick him up and take him back to the estate. They had found a nurse for the major and apologised to him for leaving but they had a duty to help a soldier of their father's brigade return home. The major was telling his parents they were in the presence of angels.

The transport of the corporal was not too much of a problem. He had lost a leg but could use a wheelchair. The twins could get him on a normal train carriage. The corporal could not believe his luck; he was leaving the hospital, being escorted to Birmingham by two beautiful young women and was going to stay at a mansion in the country. The twins were also going to take him to Bromyard; it was their duty.

All went well and a month passed by. Invitations to the wedding were sent out and the twins had been back on duty at the hospital in Birmingham. However, they decided they had to get back to visit Leicestershire; they were worried about the major. Reggie would not let them ride to Leicestershire on their own, so they had to take the groom with them. He was excited, as he had never ridden that far. Reggie was going to take care of the stables.

Two weeks after the invitations had been sent out, Reggie received a message that his uncle Albert would be in Birmingham on business and asked if they could meet at the club. Uncle Albert was Reggie's mother's elder brother and neither Reggie nor Bertie had seen him since they were young. Even though Bertie had lived in Oxford, he had not been to Uncle Albert's estate, as it was out of town. Apparently, Albert was a member of a club in Oxford that was affiliated with his own club in Birmingham. They made arrangements and when the day arrived, Nephews and Uncle met at the club and Reggie found that his Uncle Albert was in a jovial mood.

"Your mother, my sister, is a very stubborn woman. According to her, you are doing everything wrong and the twins are ruining the estate. She has decided never to visit the estate again."

"Firstly, my mother is living in the last century; she can't stand change. I think the twins prolonged my father's life and they were running the estate at a profit. They had to take their rightful place in the house and our mother was against that. You will meet them at the wedding and can then make your own judgement."

"We will all stay in a couple of hotels in Leicester and hire two coaches to bring us to the wedding and reception. Your mother will come with us to the wedding, then leave straight away for Oxford. My brother and I and our wives, will come to the reception in Birmingham and stay at a hotel."

"You could all stay on the estate; we have room," Reggie replied.

"We can discuss that prior to the wedding; now let's have a drink and toast the bride and groom."

Reggie and Bertie found that they were enjoying the company of their uncle, whom they really did not know. When the twins arrived at the major's estate, they left the groom with the major while they opened up Alice's house. The groom was tasked with pushing the major's bed onto the patio and the major took this as an opportunity to quiz him about the twins.

"How long have you known the twins?"

"They were about ten when I got the job as a groom. When they asked me something using their voices together, I was in shock. I don't remember what they asked but I am sure my answer was rubbish. They talked to the horses and I watched the horses and could see that they were listening. When they talked to the cattle, I was astonished but when they talked to the chickens, I thought it was witchcraft. I would go with His Lordship and those two young ladies to the market. They picked the cattle and the horses to buy and His Lordship would not say anything and just pay up. I remember when they bought a young bull and they told me he would make His Lordship a lot of money. I knew nothing about cattle and couldn't see how they would know anything either but they were correct. When that bull became an adult, he was making good money for his lordship. He was hired out to farmers to do his duty with the herd and the twins negotiated the price."

The major was laughing to himself as the groom spared him the gory details of the bull's exploits. The twins came back and told the groom his clothes were in the servant's quarters at Alice's house. They then took him to the stables. When they returned, the twins had an idea to buy two ponies and break them in with the help of the groom. The major insisted that he had money from his pension and money saved while in the army. He would like to pay for these horses and to do so, he would send his father to the market to pay. The twins said they might buy two dairy cattle to expand the herd; the major was in agreement. On market day, they set out early, with the groom driving and the major's father as a passenger. The twins rode by the side of the wagon. They checked out the stock and after due consideration together, without the need to speak aloud, they selected and bought two young horses, two dairy cows and two beef cattle.

The major's father reflected on his experience: "I have never been to a market to be entertained. Firstly, the cart is uncomfortable, especially for my old bones. We arrived and whenever the young ladies spoke, everyone was shocked and took a moment to answer. I think the horses and the cattle were as bemused as the people. We purchased the horses and the dairy cattle before the auction but I wanted to go to experience the auction. These young ladies told me to bid on two beef cattle and instructed me that when I reached a certain price, they would wipe their noses with a handkerchief and I should stop bidding. My heart was thumping fast because I was competing with two other bidders. When we reached a certain price, everyone was watching two ladies wipe their noses with a flourish in unison and the bidding stopped. I would have bid several pounds more but the other men stopped bidding and we got a bargain. I think the young ladies bewitched them; it was better than any theatre performance."

Alice's father never called them 'twins'; he always referred to them as 'young ladies'.

The twins were spending their days breaking in horses and nursing the major. They wanted him to be physically able to get to the church for the wedding but knew that it was going to be difficult to get him into the standard type of wheelchair available. They found that there was a man making wheelchairs in Leicester, so they rode over to see him. After his initial surprise at their identical appearance and speech, he asked how he could be of assistance to them. They told him they wanted him to design and make a chair that could be laid out like a bed. The seat should be able to rise to any height, the leg rest should be able to come up and the headrest should be lowered to create a flat surface. When transferring the patient from the bed to the wheelchair, the seat should be slightly lower and when doing the reverse, the chair should be slightly higher. The wheelchair maker thought that it could be done but wanted to see the bed and patient, so the twins said they would send the groom with a cart to fetch him the next day and a time was agreed.

The wheelchair maker arrived the next day and everyone watched with interest as he made his measurements. The twins had explained to the major what was happening and he was thinking, *These girls could be engineers.* The twins told the wheelchair maker that they would contact the local hospital to give his prototype a trial in a real-world setting. The man went away with a generous deposit and he made a promise to give the job top priority. He was good at his word and within a week, the chair was ready.

At the trial test, they had the matron, nurses and two doctors standing by. Two orderlies were ready to pull the sheet under a patient to lift him onto the wheelchair. The chair was positioned with the bed flat and the patient was deposited on the new bed. Then the back was raised and the footrest lowered. The whole ward was clapping as this procedure took place, including the patients. The twins spoke to tell them this bed was designed to get their uncle to a wedding. It went very quiet and so the matron told them they could cheer. The wheelchair maker was asking whether he could copy their design and make more and they told him that, of course, he could; he was the maker and they were only nurses.

After a week, the time came to trial the new device with the major in a real-life situation. The major could put no pressure on his legs but could raise his torso for a short while. He was often in some pain but would not let the twins know. The twins and the groom used his bed sheet and positioned him on the chair. His father and mother were watching nervously, with their fingers crossed. They wheeled him to the front door and suddenly realised there were steps. The major said he thought there would be a problem but then he regretted that he had spoken in haste and would appear to be ungrateful. The twins said they would design a ramp and his father said he knew a carpenter who would build the ramp. Within a few days, the ramp had been constructed and the problem had been overcome.

The major was so happy he was mobile, with the groom initially pushing him until he got the hang of propelling himself. His first journey was to the stables, as he wanted to talk to the horses. The twins advised him to talk softly and the interested horses would come to him. The one horse that did not come to him was his own horse. He was disappointed but the twins told the major that maybe he should talk louder to his horse and in a more commanding voice. It worked and the major was once again telling himself that the twins were magicians.

The groom was greatly enjoying his time in Leicestershire. He was sleeping alone in a big house. All his meals were at the estate house. The garden at Alice's house needed a bit of work but he could get vegetables for the cook. She was giving him plenty of food, including pastries, his favourite. He had many discussions with the major and they became friends. In the evening, there was a pub near the house or he could read books from an extensive library. Of course, like all good things, it had to come to an end. Reggie sent word that he wanted the groom to come back to his estate to look after the stables, as Reggie was heavily involved with the wedding preparations and could no longer afford the time. The groom had a good send-off for his long ride back to Birmingham. He was invited to come back any time he could.

The twins had moved the sewing machine into the major's room so they could work and talk to him at the same time. They were making their bridesmaids' dresses and the major was enjoying a fashion show almost every day. The twins found the new wheelchair very useful for changing the bed sheets and cleaning the major. He had very quickly lost his bashfulness and the twins just took on their nursing tasks as normal. The major's mother was taken aback by the nature of these chores but on consideration, she realised they had to be done and the twins were doing a good job. The major's father thought they could do the muckiest job and still remain cheerful.

When the carpenter made the ramp, the twins had asked him to build another hen house; they were keen on increasing the egg production. They had then bought some more hens and Alice's father was watching the egg production increase. They did not have to sell the eggs at the market, as they had talked a man into coming to the estate to buy the eggs. He was delighted with the egg production but on his daily visits, he became fascinated with the twins talking to the hens. Was the high egg production linked to their talking? This was the question he kept asking himself.

The wedding was fast approaching and the church was too far away for the major to propel himself to the church. The twins had to devise a way to get his chair onto a cart. At the church, they would then get local men to lift the chair and the major off the cart; he was a hero in the village, so there would be no problem finding men for this task. The carpenter built a ramp to a platform about the height of a cart. The girls did a dummy run without the major and it worked well. The major's father was watching these developments on his estate, shaking his head at their ingenuity and enjoying everything new.

Two days before the wedding, Reggie, Alice, Bertie, Elsie and Benjamin arrived. They would all be staying in Alice's house, except Alice herself, who would stay with her parents and the twins. Benjamin was growing and immediately recognised the twins. He pointed to Agnes and said her name; he then pointed to Elizabeth and said her name. Elsie was bemused; she could not pick them apart to name them; the twins were delighted; Benjamin was the only one who could pick them.

At dinner on the estate, the major sat at the table in his wheelchair. Reggie was marvelling at the major's improvement and counting his own blessings that he had never been shot. He was not sure that he would have the grit or courage that the major had shown. Reggie asked whether the twins had made any improvements to the estate. Alice's father was gushing in his praise of the twins, as their selling horses, buying cattle and buying chickens had made this much more profit in a few months than ever before. The major chimed in to say that Reggie was lucky in that he had produced farmers, horse trainers, nurses and engineers, all in two girls. Even then, he thought he must have forgotten something.

    The twins were keen to get Alice alone; they wanted to see her wedding dress. The ladies retired to Alice's room, where they all dressed for the wedding. Alice loved the bridesmaid's dresses and admitted her dress had been designed and made in Birmingham. Alice was praising them for all they had done for her brother and her parents. They told her in some ways that they liked this estate better than the one in Birmingham.

    The big day came and the twins busied themselves helping the major on to the cart. He was telling them to relax and just be bridesmaids. Alice was nervous; the twins were nervous but Alice's mother was an ocean of calm. She told them all to relax and that the real pressure came after the wedding. Entering the church, it seemed that more people were looking at the twins rather than the bride. Alice's relatives had not seen them before and likewise, Reggie's relatives from Oxford had never seen them.

    The twins had not seen the major taken from the cart but after the ceremony, which went well, they were keen observers of the major being lifted back onto the cart. Their grandmother had tersely nodded to them but then ignored them completely. They wanted to talk to her but she was not going to communicate. Bertie was watching and decided his mother was a lost cause. After the ceremony, everyone except her ladyship retired to the estate. She wished Reggie and Alice a happy marriage and then immediately departed for Leicester.

Alice's mother had decided that a long table with no chairs at the table but chairs placed around the room, was the best way to make the families mix. The major's bed had been pushed into a corner to make more space. The long table was full of food and the major noted there were several egg dishes, hopefully made with produce from his estate. The twins were meeting lots of new relatives and of course, their unified speech had everyone stunned. Bertie brought his uncle Albert to meet them. He had heard them speak during the afternoon but he was still taken aback. Albert was keen to talk to them about running an estate. He felt that his sister had exaggerated about their competence but he wanted to talk to the twins to see firsthand what they knew. Bertie was watching as the twins gave his uncle a lecture on how to run an estate. Alice's father also chimed in to tell Albert about how the twins had changed his estate vastly for the better. The festivities ended and Reggie told them they would reconvene at his estate in Birmingham in three days. He would be very pleased if his uncles came.

The major said he wanted to also go to the estate in three days and the twins told him it would be a very long journey but they were willing to ride with him. His parents were going by train and after some discussion, it was decided that rather than go by cart, he would also go by train. The twins were going to stay and go on the train with the major. They knew that at the train stations there would be porters to lift the major on and off a cart. At Leicester, the twins were finding their carriage when the major came along the platform in his wheelchair; he had arranged to be taken off the cart and was well pleased with himself.

At Birmingham, two porters took him from the train and deposited him on the platform. Outside the station, Reggie had sent a carriage and a cart to take everyone to the estate. The twins found two large porters and asked them to lift the major onto the cart. The porters were momentarily in shock at the unified speech of these two young ladies and then one porter asked if the ladies could say that again. There was a lot of laughter; they spoke again and Agnes tipped the porters. After their task was completed, the porters said that they hoped the twins would come back soon and talk to them.

Arriving on the estate, the twins remembered that there was a flight of stairs to the main door, so they needed to enter through the kitchen. All the living quarters were on the second floor and the major would have to sleep in the servant's quarters. The major told them that being near the kitchen was a bonus. He was going to have their old room and would have easy access to the grounds. Reggie had greeted his in-laws and then came to the kitchen to greet his daughters and his brother-in-law. He said they should toast the occasion and that he had a special drink. Reggie explained that when he returned from the wedding, there was a present for the two young ladies; it was a small barrel of cider from the corporal in Bromyard. He could not resist trying the cider; it was very good. Two large glasses and two small glasses were poured. Reggie said they had to taste their cider but he was afraid that he would probably drink most of it. They said they liked it but it was strong; they cautioned their father about drinking too much. Reggie and the major were laughing at this and Reggie told his brother-in-law that in all his time in the army, no one had cautioned him about drinking too much—in fact, quite the opposite.

The twins left to greet their new stepmother and the men had another sample of the cider. Reggie was asking himself why they were always confined to the upper floor. The major said he wanted to see the stables and Reggie was only too happy to push him to see the horses. The major was admiring Reggie's horse and Reggie told him that when he called the horse, there was a moment of hesitation. If the girls called the horse, he reacted immediately. There were lots of instances when the twins had more power or authority than he did but he felt that they had earned it.

Alice was very pleased to see the twins; there were lots of hugs and kisses. Alice had never felt so free with other ladies. Her father and mother were admiring the estate. The twins said if they wished, they would get a tour. Alice's father was asking himself whether anyone had ever offered him a tour. Alice's mother was keen on seeing her son and so they all retired to the kitchen. The old cook said she had never had so many people in her kitchen but they should know that His Lordship was in the stables. They all walked to the stables to see the men grooming the horses.

Reggie was very happy with his new brother-in-law and said after the reception that he should stay as long as he liked. Alice was watching her brother and husband together; she could not be happier with the way they interacted. The twins were tending to their uncle at the time and were delighted with his pleasure. They knew their new grandparents would leave after the reception, so they asked if the groom could go with them to look after their estate. Reggie was asking himself why he had never thought of that.

Reggie told his two uncles not to stay in Birmingham; he had plenty of room in his house. Bertie was starting to enjoy his uncles and realised his mother had taken them out of his reach. The two uncles, Albert and Lionel, were very different from their sister, his mother. They were quite knowledgeable but much more receptive to new ideas. Their two estates were quite close to Oxford and they would often meet in the men's club and inevitably, much of their discussion was about their stubborn sister.

The reception started on the second floor but soon gravitated to the ground floor, where the twins were with the major. Reggie was telling Alice he was sorry but his daughters were a drawing card. She was laughing and saying her brother was the drawing card. Actually, the cider was also a drawing card; all the men almost never drank cider but they were very much enjoying this dwindling supply. Reggie decided that he was going to order another barrel after the reception.

Reggie's uncles were fascinated with the twins talking to the animals, even the hens. The twins told them the cockerel was a little stubborn but he would occasionally come when they called. All the men were laughing at the concept of a stubborn cockerel. Meanwhile, most of the ladies were upstairs, enjoying their time without the men. Finally, the twins said they should be with the ladies. All the men were loath to let them go. Albert said he was going to invite the twins to his estate, as he was very interested in their farming ideas. Bertie was smiling at the twins getting all the accolades; he had known that from an early age these girls would be stars.

The reception was over and the guests left for home. The cider had been well and truly finished and Reggie was going to have to order another barrel. The twins suggested they take the major on a train trip and get another barrel of cider while returning the empty. Reggie was a bit hesitant but the twins had talked Alice into supporting their idea. Once Alice said it was a good idea, Reggie said yes. The twins hired a carpenter to make a ramp to a platform the same height as the cart and then they were prepared to show the major sights of Birmingham. The first place they went was the hospital. The matron was so glad to see them and warmly welcomed the major. They went to the soldier's ward and the patients started cheering. The major was getting emotional, so they introduced him to the soldiers and then it was all talk about where they had served and where and when they were injured. The twins were watching their uncle get attention and they were so happy. The major was also enjoying himself.

The porters at the station were very pleased to see the twins again and lifted the major off the cart with pleasure. They followed the wheelchair to the carriage and lifted him from the platform. The twins gave them a tip and the porters said they would do it for free; they just wanted to hear them speak. Bromyard station had the two large porters and after a bit of a delay hearing the twins speak, the major was on his way to the brewery. The cart driver was just shaking his head as they headed for the farm; he seemed almost afraid to speak.

The corporal was sitting at a desk outside the brew house when the twins arrived. He jumped up, grabbed his crutch and despite his injuries, was beside the cart before they knew it. The major was lifted off the cart and given a tour of the brewery. The empty barrel was returned and the twins thanked the corporal but they must pay for a larger barrel. They explained that their father liked the cider and the major negotiated the cost of sending a barrel on a regular basis to his local in Leicestershire.

The corporal wanted to give them a reduction in price but the twins told him their father was paying and would probably drink most of the cider. The major told the twins he was treated like royalty in the brewery and one or two men bowed to him. The twins humorously apologised for not curtseying to him.

"Maybe you could do that in the future."

The twins frowned at this and the major said he was only joking and then he roared with laughter. They said to themselves that he must have had some cider in the brewery. Arriving back on the estate, they were met by an excited uncle, Bertie. The Oxford family wanted to see the twins. Uncle Albert had invited the twins to his estate along with Bertie, Elsie and Benjamin. Apparently, Benjamin entertained the aunties almost as much as the twins. The twins loved Benjamin and did not mind being upstaged by a small boy. Reggie was very pleased with his new cider barrel and the news about the trip to Bromyard.

The following week, Bertie took the carriage and they all set out for Oxford. Bertie had done this trip several times when he was at university but never as the driver. Bertie said they would stop at Stratford-upon-Avon for an early lunch. Benjamin was talking to the twins one at a time. They loved this cousin and he was not fazed by them talking in unison. Elsie was riding up front with Bertie, so Benjamin had the twins all to himself. He was continually pointing to new things and there was animated conversation in the carriage. They stopped at Stratford; the ordering of lunch and the speech of the twins caused the normal palaver. Elsie was always surprised by people's reactions but Bertie and even Benjamin seemed to expect it.

The drive from Stratford to Oxford was long but on a decent road. Bertie was getting used to driving the carriage and was enjoying himself. In Oxford, which was a scenic delight, they obtained directions to Albert's estate. Arriving at the estate, there was a large welcoming committee but no grandmother. As soon as the twins spoke, a hush came over the gathering. Uncle Albert was the first to speak after the silence and said that even though he had warned everyone, the old saying was true; it had to be seen and heard to be believed.

Bertie met several cousins, who were second cousins to the twins. Albert had listened to his sister tell him about Reggie's outrageous seating plan and decided to try it at dinner that night. His wife sat on his left and the twins were on his right. His brother sat at the end of the table with Bertie and Benjamin and Elsie sat next to his wife. Albert loved this informality. His wife was preoccupied with Benjamin, so he could talk all the time to the twins.

The next day at breakfast, Albert told the guests and family that they could sit anywhere; he decided not to sit at the head of the table and he was enjoying breakfast as never before. The servants seemed a bit perplexed. Bertie told his uncle he would like to see his mother.

"Do not worry; I told her she must come to dinner tonight and if she does not come, we will all descend on her house."

Bertie loved this side of his uncle and was regretting the time he had spent in Oxford without contacting this family. After breakfast, they all adjourned to the stables, a place Albert's wife rarely visited. The twins were talking to the horses and doing their normal tricks; Albert's wife was asking whether this was magic or witchcraft.

"They are just talking to the horse and the horses are listening. I suppose they are mesmerised or maybe it is witchcraft." Albert was laughing to himself.

The twins said there was one horse not listening; he was a stallion and maybe it was because he was male. Now everyone was laughing. The twins said they would spend some time with him and ride him tomorrow. Albert knew this was a difficult horse and the twins had identified that in a matter of minutes. These girls certainly had a gift for understanding horses. Off they went then to view the dairy herd. Albert made cheese and butter on the estate and the excess was sold in Oxford.

By this time, Lionel had arrived and when he watched the twins talk to the cattle, he was fascinated. Lionel was told that at dinner tonight, their sister would sit between them and the twins would sit opposite their grandmother. Bertie would sit at the head of the table; Albert had never sat in the middle of the table since he was a child and he was excited. Lionel was still watching the twins talk to the cattle.

Her ladyship arrived just before dinner and was greeted by the twins, who gave her a peck on the cheek. She was taken aback when she was sitting between her brothers, who were not sitting in their customary positions at the head of the table. Albert had to restrain himself from laughing; his sister was so stuck in old-fashioned ways.

The twins were sitting opposite their grandmother and they were flanked by Albert and Lionel's wives. Bertie and Elsie were sitting at the head of the table. To her ladyship, it was all wrong and her elder brother was doing this on purpose to upset her. Lionel was quietly laughing and when the discussion about talking to animals started, he thought he might have to leave the table before he disgraced himself by guffawing like a dolt. Albert was praising the twins as being expert estate managers, which clearly made her ladyship uncomfortable.

Lionel said he had pigs and the twins told him they were difficult to train.

"You mean you talk to pigs?" her ladyship said indignantly.

"Yes, pigs are highly intelligent and can be stubborn, grandmother."

Now everyone was laughing and her ladyship realised she had been out manoeuvred. The whole table was now discussing animals. Bertie was watching and knew the twins would get the better of his mother. The dinner went very well after the initial discussions. Lionel talked to Bertie later and said this was the best dinner party he had ever attended. Albert had put on a unique seating plan that worked and he had watched his elder sister get more and more uncomfortable. When the talk turned to pigs, he said that he thought he might have to leave the table; he had visions of his old pigs, listening to no man, let alone obeying. He told Bertie they must come to his estate the next day; he could send a carriage for them. Bertie explained they had a carriage of their own and he was now used to driving.

Lionel, being the second son, did not inherit his parent's estate but he had married a lady who was an only child and so he had inherited her estate. Bertie observed them to be a very loving couple who talked and laughed a lot together. Lionel's estate had a large piggery as well as dairy cows; he also had a herd of goats, which was unusual for this part of England. The twins were intrigued by the goats but Lionel was insistent that they talk to the pigs first. Everyone was watching from a distance as the twins started to talk to the pigs. The old pigs were ignoring them completely but a couple of younger pigs took an interest. The twins manoeuvred them to one end of the piggery and then others followed; finally, the old pigs came to investigate. The twins explained they would have to give the pigs names and that could take time. Lionel said that was enough and his wife was laughing and hugging the twins.

Benjamin had been watching his cousins and also wanted to talk to the pigs. Elsie told Bertie, who said Benjamin was copying his cousins and why not let him try? The twins returned from the goats and watched their cousin talk to the pigs, which made them very happy. They told Lionel that the goats could be difficult. The twins' identical appearance did not seem to have the same visual effect on the goats. Once they attracted their attention, their speech had an effect. They thought that maybe, because many goats looked similar, two human twins did not seem so unusual. Lionel had never really looked closely at his goats and now he had a new project: to observe his goats.

Lionel called them in for pre-lunch drinks, saying that he had cider for the men if they wished. He told Bertie that he had only drunk cider when he was young but now he had discovered some good stuff around Oxford; he thanked Reggie for his reintroduction to the drink.

Lionel showed the visitors around his house and the twins were interested in the artefacts sent from India. Lionel's eldest son was in India with the British Administration. Lionel showed them maps of India and the twins decided they would like to travel there. Lionel advised them not to go to India as the diseases there were killers and he was constantly afraid for his son.

The dinner that night also had an unusual seating plan but this was not fully implemented as her ladyship had called off her attendance, as she had another appointment already planned. Lionel thought two dinners in an uncomfortable situation were too much for his sister. The conversation at the dinner was lively. The twins were talking to Lionel's second son and Lionel watched as his son was overawed by these two ladies. Bertie and Elsie were talking to their son, who said he thought he could talk to pigs. Benjamin wandered over to talk to his cousins and Bertie was telling Elsie that maybe the twins had given him a gift. Lionel's wife loved wandering around the room, talking to anyone. Normally, she would sit in one place and others would come and talk to her.

They stayed overnight at Lionel's mansion and in the morning Benjamin refused to eat any bacon. The twins told him that this pig was very old and had to be killed for its own good. Benjamin ate the bacon. Lionel watched and listened with interest and this episode had him thinking about where he sold his animals. After breakfast, everyone adjourned to the stables. Lionel's second son told the twins that there was one horse that seemed completely untrainable. He pointed out the horse that was in its stall, so the twins approached this horse. He was a stallion who was trying to show he was the boss. The twins talked to each other and then they talked in unison; they spoke quietly and saw the horse trying to listen. They then separated and talked in unison. The horse was looking from one to the other; he was confused. The twins then approached and stroked his forehead while talking in unison. The horse calmed down and they let him out of his stall and walked him to the paddock. The audience was silent and still at this development, except Benjamin, who rushed over to his cousins and hugged them. They lifted Benjamin up and introduced him to Major, a name they had just christened the horse.

Elsie had her heart in her mouth at this development and Lionel's wife was again asking herself whether this was magic or witchcraft (similar to Albert's wife). Lionel wanted to say something but the words would not come. Agnes calmly put a saddle on the horse; Elizabeth mounted and took Major for a ride. She came back and picked up Benjamin, placed him on the saddle in front of her and went for another ride. Bertie nodded his approval and told Elsie that these cousins would never put Benjamin in harm's way. Lionel finally found his voice and was telling everyone he had never seen horsemanship like this before. His wife corrected him and said it was a horsewoman ship.

"I don't care what you call it; I call it a miracle."

Benjamin was telling his cousins he wanted to ride like them and he also wanted to talk to horses. They promised they would get him a small pony and teach him to ride. Bertie closed his eyes and was silently thanking Sally for sending the best nieces in the world. Later, Benjamin indeed received a small horse but it was not a pony but a fully grown miniature horse.

The twins returned to the estate and reported all this news to their father. Reggie was told that he should be expecting regular visits from his uncles from this point on. Bertie told him about the dinner parties and Reggie was laughing at his mother's discomfort. Now he said that he had to concentrate on running the estate and finding the twins some other employment. They did not need to work to earn money but he felt that they needed to get out of the estate and spread their wings to see more of the wider world. At the club, one of his army friends said they might join the military nursing corps. Reggie could only suggest it to the twins and let them make up their own minds.

Meanwhile, the twins returned to the estate, which resulted in a party with music, dancing and singing. They watched Alice, who seemed to be enjoying everything but not entering into the dancing. The twins suspected something. The following day, they were sitting with her when they asked, "Are you pregnant?"

"I may be; I am not sure but tell no one, especially Reggie."

"Let us say we are very excited but only you should tell our father."

The twins went back to their room and were asking themselves all sorts of questions. Alice was not too old to have a baby but death in childbirth had to be considered. To the twins, the thought of losing Alice was unthinkable but they still thought about it. It could be a baby brother or a baby sister; they did not care. If he were a boy, he would inherit the estate; they did not care. Could Alice have twins? That would be a miracle but the very thought was worth considering and relishing. In the morning, the twins told each other that they had both experienced a sleepless night and that they should go talk to the animals. They needed to be distracted from all these possibilities.

Reggie was travelling a lot but Alice was happy to stay at home. He had been to Newcastle to see a sergeant. He had been to Bromyard to enjoy the cider. He was very welcome in Leicestershire and had spent a few days with his brother-in-law and his parents-in-law. At his club in London, he was discussing his daughters with a military doctor, who told him his daughters should join the military nursing unit. The doctor was expecting a war soon and nurses would be sorely needed. Reggie thought he could only suggest his daughters should join the military and see what they thought of the idea.

Alice was indeed pregnant and now that Reggie knew, the twins were rejoicing at every opportunity. Benjamin was a bit confused by all of this, so they explained that their love for him would not change but he might have someone to play with but they were not sure whether it would be a girl or a boy. The twins sat down and admitted to themselves that what they had told Benjamin was confusing. Bertie was able to explain the situation to Benjamin, who then explained it to his cousins. His cousins listened quietly and thanked him for the information. This conversation made them love Benjamin even more.

Reggie suggested to the girls that they join a military nursing unit. If they did not like the discipline in the army, they could always come back to the estate. The twins had often talked about nursing in the army. Their uncle (Alice's brother) had suggested it sometime before and now they were going to do it. They thought they should not delay, even though they wanted to see through the duration of Alice's confinement. Joining the army meant they were immediately sent to London.

The matron of the Mile End Military Hospital in London greeted two new nurses and got a shock. It took her several seconds to react.

"Do you always speak like that and how can I tell which is Agnes and which is Elizabeth?"

"We speak in unison and when we are apart, the other knows what her twin said. Agnes wears a badge on the right side."

"Well, that will help; we now have to find you identical uniforms and put the badge on one. I see you have served in a hospital in Birmingham. I know that, matron, for we trained together. I will give her a call and have a talk."

The matron called a senior sister to take the twins to see the quartermaster. The twins did not speak until they met the quartermaster. The senior sister and the quartermaster were speechless for a while. After the initial shock, they received uniforms that might need a bit of alterations but they told the quartermaster they could do their own alterations. The senior sister said she would take them around the wards but warned them that some of the soldier's language could not be nice.

"We are used to talking to ordinary soldiers and our father tells us the soldiers moderate their language when we are around."

As they entered the ward, it went silent and one man shouted, "Will one of you marry me?"

"If you have a twin, we might consider it."

Of course, they spoke in unison and it took several seconds for the room to erupt in laughter. They approached one man with an obvious abdominal wound and told him his laughter must be giving him pain. It took him about a minute to answer.

"I can stand the pain but I have not laughed for a long time and it is worth the pain."

All the patients in the ward started clapping. The senior sister went back to the matron to report a miracle.

A ward where it was hard to get a few words from the patients was now a place full of laughter. She had left the twins telling the patients about talking to animals. When they were speaking, the room was silent and every man was listening. She had to get back to take the twins to see the officers. The matron had talked to her friend in Birmingham and was told similar stories to the ones her senior sister had told her. Having just joined the army, they were appointed as staff nurses but if they showed how to treat wounds, she would promote them to sisters (equivalent to a lieutenant in the army).

The officers were just as surprised by these new nurses and the twins told them their father was a brigadier and their uncle was a major; both had served in South Africa. Once over their shock, the officers had lots of questions. They were surprised at the knowledge the twins had of the world; they had never met young ladies like these two. The senior sister came and apologised to the officers for taking the twins away. They were taken to the matron, who said they had no specific duties at this time but if they could go to all the wards and cheer up the soldiers, she would be very happy. She wanted to see how they bandaged wounds but that could wait until the end of the week.

The weeks passed and the twins were promoted. Several senior officers came to visit the matron; they had heard about these new nurses. Finally, a general came and said he wanted these nurses to visit all the military hospitals, as it would be good for morale. The twins visited the wards and told the soldiers they were off to Scotland but they would be back. They were applauded in every ward as they departed. The matron told them the general had planned their journey and that they were going to visit many hospitals and that in a way, she was envious of their opportunity. The twins learned there were many military hospitals in the United Kingdom and there were also civilian hospitals with wounded soldiers.

They were picked up by a swanky staff car and the matron said that it must belong to a general. The train journey to Edinburgh was quite long but they had comfortable seats in First Class. They pointed at the menus for their meal but had to reply when they were asked if they wanted wine. Their unison reply of 'No Thank You' had the waiter rooted to the spot for at least a minute. He finally asked the question again and apologised, saying that he wanted to hear them answer together.

At Edinburgh, they were met by the matron of the military hospital, who could not wait to meet them. She had been warned of their 'unison speak' but was still surprised when they spoke. This matron had a strong Scottish accent and the twins asked her whether they could try to copy her speech and hoped they were not too impertinent. She told them to go ahead and then these twins showed they could copy her accent exactly. She was laughing and said they should try that in the wards, as they would hear some very strong accents and even new words. The matron could not wait to get them to the hospital but asked if they needed rest. Their reply was that the train journey was a rest.

Entering the soldiers' ward, there was silence, as someone had let them know they were going to be visited by some interesting nurses. They said, "Good evening, gentlemen," and there was silence. Then they repeated the greeting with a Scottish accent and after a short silence, the room erupted into cheering. The matron was watching this development with a tear in her eye. The twins moved around the ward, talking to wounded soldiers and were indeed amazed at the range of different accents. The matron told the soldiers these new nurses needed a rest but they would be back tomorrow. One soldier shouted something the twins did not understand and the matron said it was Gaelic. The soldier was telling the matron to keep her promise. They visited a couple of more hospitals in Edinburgh and after a couple of weeks, the twins moved to Glasgow to be confronted by even more different Scottish accents.

The soldiers in Glasgow seemed less reserved than those in Edinburgh. They entered one ward to be confronted by a soldier shouting, 'We wear nothing under the kilt.'

"Well, we are sure that keeps you cool in the summer but we hate to think about the winter."

There was silence for about a minute and then the room erupted in laughter. After that episode, there was no bad language.

The twins started to realise that in a large city like Glasgow, there were several hospitals that had wounded soldiers. They were able to use military transport to visit quite a few hospitals. This was because the general was getting lots of reports about their visits and they were all good. The twins were doing little nursing and plenty of entertaining. In Liverpool, they had their first sight of the sea and they got to talk to wounded sailors. These sailors were astonished at the twin's geographical knowledge.

Next stop was Birmingham, where they visited a few hospitals, especially the one where they had first been introduced to nursing. The matron was receiving regular reports of their adventures and as a result, she had renewed her friendship with the matron at Mile End; she was soon going to spend a week with her in London. During their time in Birmingham, the twins had two weeks of leave and of course; they went to visit the estate.

Reggie and Alice were so glad to see them and there was a lot of hugging and kissing. Bertie and Elsie provided a similar welcome. Benjamin immediately identified each twin by name and told them not to speak in unison; he wanted to talk to them individually and do the same with his kisses. To the twins, this little boy was special and they would let him have a few liberties, so they parted and told him to make his choice.

He looked at them and said, "I love you both equally, so get together so that I can kiss you both at the same time."

Watching on, the audience was close to tears.

Now they had to meet their new baby brother. While they were away, Alice had delivered a large baby boy into the world; Reggie and Alice had named him Arthur, the name of the sergeant Reggie had sent to Newcastle. When Reggie told his mother she was disgusted with such a thing, declaring it "most common," Alice said she loved the name and that it was her father's third name.

Arthur was asleep when the twins approached his cot but he awoke, looked at them and smiled. Both Agnes and Elizabeth found that they had tears trickling down their cheeks but smiled back. Arthur gurgled something and the twins copied him, he smiled. The audience was mesmerised and the twins asked Alice whether they could hold him. Alice thought he might start crying, as he did not often like to be held. There was no crying problem and the twins gently kissed Arthur. Reggie had to leave the room at this point, as here were his children meeting for the first time and getting to know each other; he found the sight to him extremely emotional. The age discrepancy was large but that did not matter; they were all of his blood.

The next morning at breakfast, Alice told them she had a pram on the ground floor and Arthur loved his pram. The twins could hardly finish their breakfast quickly enough and had Arthur in the pram as soon as they could. They took Arthur to meet the horses and the horses were glad to see them. Arthur was lifted up and encouraged to stroke the horses. The twins were telling each other that their brother had to love horses and be a good rider.

They had not seen their father at breakfast and thought it was their duty to find him and greet him. Reggie was pondering some news from Europe. The Kaiser, who was the late queen's nephew, was building a large army. Reggie was still in regular contact with his army colleagues and was getting lots of intelligence reports. The twins interrupted his thoughts and each gave him a kiss. He was glad they took his thoughts away from a potential war. They were telling him they were in love with their brother and hoping he would be as intelligent as Benjamin. Reggie loved Benjamin and every time he saw him, he would have a laugh. Arthur was too young yet but he was hoping his son would also give him plenty of laughs.

The twins were discussing their hospital visits and telling Reggie about the different military hospitals. Benjamin joined them, for he had heard their voices as he freely roamed around the house. He asked where they were going next. They told him Aldershot first and then back to London.

"They do a lot of marching there; I hope the soldiers will help you."

"Nurses do not march and it is the reverse; we are there to help the soldiers."

Reggie was having a good laugh. He could imagine a drill sergeant being forced into silence when they spoke to him. His daughters were going to have a very different experience in the army and in a way, he was envious.

Leaving the estate for Aldershot was a kissing and hugging event on a grand scale, with plenty of tears. At

Aldershot, they saw a lot of marching and were told by one of the doctors that the army was preparing for war. The Kaiser had built a large army and most people suspected the Germans could be a formidable opponent. The doctor said that he thought they should go back to their base in London as quickly as possible. On their return to London, they found that the matron was eagerly awaiting their arrival to cheer up her hospital. She was resisting the general's attempt to send them to other hospitals south of London. What they did not know was that the general and Reggie were friends and Reggie had suggested the twins could cheer up dour military hospitals.

    After the girls had spent a couple of months in London, the general got his way and they were on their way to Portsmouth. In Portsmouth, they saw some very large ships, including a hospital ship. This was a commandeered liner that had been converted into a hospital ship and the twins were thrilled to be invited aboard to see the facilities. Even in the harbour, this ship was rocking and the twins wondered what it would be like to take the vessel out to sea in a gale. The captain, after his initial shock, invited them to lunch. He was not a military man but his second in command was a captain and a doctor. The twins were thrilled to listen to these men tell them about life at sea. The captain was surprised at their knowledge of geography. The doctor was delighted at their knowledge of wounds and how to treat them. A tour of the ship was a delight for the twins, who imagined the challenges of treating injured soldiers on the high seas and whether this would lie in their futures.

From Portsmouth, they were off to Plymouth, where they saw more ships and had the delight of being taken by boat out into the channel. Army transport was enlisted to take the twins on a tour of Devon and Cornwall, with plenty of time to see the rugged coastline and also Dartmoor prison (from the outside). They loved seeing horses on the moors but they had no chance to ride. Their visit to several small hospitals was a delight to all concerned. They cheered up the patients and there always seemed to be a wounded soldier or two from the Boer War. While they were in Plymouth, war with Germany was declared. There was a lot of army movement and a sense of urgency, so they had to wait a few days for transport. They did not mind, as they were enjoying the fresh sea air and were fascinated by the army and navy movements. Finally, they were able to solve the army transport problem by getting a train back to London, they made their own way from the station to the hospital; their luggage would follow them later.

The matron was so happy to see them; some of the nurses had already been sent over to France and she was short-staffed. Many of their duties meant they were not working together but even apart; they were always communicating. One day, the matron called them to her office and told them the army was setting up a hospital in Cairo. She had received orders for the transfer of the girls; they would go as senior sisters, which was a promotion and equivalent to the rank of a captain in the army. The matron told them the fighting would be between the Turks and Empire soldiers. She said that much of this would be carried out by cavalry; she knew of their love of horses. The hospital in Cairo was to be established in a commandeered hotel but as of yet, it was not staffed. The high temperature could be a factor in their working conditions but she was sure they would manage. She said that she was very sorry to see them go but she thought this posting was better than France or Belgium.

The twins accepted immediately and went to write letters to their father and Uncle Bertie. They were excited; Uncle Bertie had told them about Africa when they were young and they had read about Egypt in their grandfather's books. The matron was unhappy to see them leave and on her request; they did a last tour of the wards because the hospital was already receiving newly injured soldiers. She warned them that this new hospital already had only a few patients but that when they arrived in Cairo; she expected there would be more, as the Turks were on the side of the Germans and the conflict would spread to the region. They were given one week's leave and would then go by ship from Portsmouth to Cairo.

Back on the estate, Arthur recognised them immediately and Benjamin was excited to find out his cousins were going to Africa. Uncle Bertie had his hands full answering the many questions that the girls had for him. Reggie had never been to Cairo but had a lot of information from friends who had been there. He told them he had seen the desert in South Africa but only from afar. He said they should see the pyramids but expect the climate to be warm and in the summer to be very warm indeed. Alice was asking whether they really wanted to go. She was hearing dreadful stories about the war in Europe. Elsie was more down to earth, saying they should go and 'take care of our boys'. That was indeed the twins' sentiment; wounded soldiers far from home had to have the best care. Benjamin asked an interesting question: "How could you have a British hospital in a foreign land?" The twins told him they were not sure but would write him a letter with the details when they saw how it all worked. This little boy was far advanced for his age and that was probably due to Bertie.

They arrived in Portsmouth to board a medium-sized passenger ship. This ship was carrying soldiers to Egypt and would not stop before Cairo. It would be escorted on the voyage by a destroyer. The twins were assigned a cabin meant for four but had it to themselves, as the other nurses were of lower rank and had a communal cabin. They had decided to speak individually, as they wanted to board without any problem. They actually found 'one-only' speaking difficult. A steward came to their cabin and gave them a timetable of meals and their first lunch would be at the captain's table. Elizabeth took the schedule and thanked the steward. At lunch, they approached the captain's table and he stood and saluted.

"Thank you, sir; we do not require a salute but appreciate your gesture."

The captain stood rooted to the spot and it took him a few moments before he spoke. The other officers at the table were equally lost for words.

"I was told you were different but no one told me how different. I am going to have firm words with my informants."

Now the whole table was full of laughter. The captain called over his steward and whispered that these ladies had to sit at his table for every meal. The initial silence was broken when the twins started to talk about their experiences in military hospitals. The captain said that was not his favourite subject but the ladies had broken the ice. The twins were telling this table of army and navy officers about injured soldiers and sailors. They soon realised that this topic was not so good at lunchtime and they quickly changed the subject. The topic was shifted to horses and they told the officers they talked to horses and could ride as good as any man. One officer asked whether the horses actually listened; they told him that not only horses but also cattle listened and that on the whole, pigs were difficult. The whole table was laughing.

The twins apologised as they felt that they may be monopolising the conversation. The captain told them to just keep talking. The stewards had the first course ready to serve but no one wanted to eat yet; they were too intent on listening to these young ladies. One officer asked about their father and where they lived. They then told them about his service in South Africa and that he was a brigadier. This lunch passed very quickly and the captain commented that he could not wait for dinner. The whole voyage was full of the twins, mesmerising their audience of army and navy officers. Hospitals were not normally a topic for the dinner table but the twins had them all listening and asking questions.

Early in the voyage, the twins were able to gather the nurses together in the wardroom and after the initial shock of hearing the twins speak in unison; the nurses asked them many questions. Some of these nurses were new to the army and lacked nursing experience. The twins enlisted one of the army officers and demonstrated bandaging arm and leg wounds on him. This officer was delighted at this role; he had never been in the company of so many young ladies. The captain was seen taking a slight peek into the room; it looked like he approved of the demonstration. Once the nurses became used to the twins, they had many questions. The twins asked the captain that evening if he could seat a couple of nurses at his table to even out the numbers. He had no problem and said that he looked forward to this new arrangement. The captain was amusing himself quietly with the thought that the twins had taken over the running of parts of his ship. The first two nurses were overawed by being situated at the captain's table, so the twins then introduced the captain and told the nurses to tell him where they were from. The captain had never been introduced at his own table; this was something new. Everyone enjoyed that meal and the discussion. The nurses entered into most of the conversation and the captain was telling himself that in the future, he would always have ladies at his table.

As they came into the harbour near Cairo, the captain was wishing this voyage had been longer. They had a smooth passage and good company and there were no encounters with enemy ships. He allowed the nurses to disembark first and the soldiers and navy crew nearby were standing to attention and saluting. The twins told the captain that if they ever came back to England from Cairo, it would be on his ship. The captain was smiling and replied that he was also hoping the twins could do another journey with him.

The twins had been at the rail when they docked in Cairo; they observed that this was human chaos on a grand scale. There seemed to be people everywhere and they were going in all directions, seemingly with little, if any, sense of order or purpose. It was also extremely hot, as when they docked, the ship halted and the sea breeze stopped. The nurses were escorted to a waiting car and a covered lorry. The other nurses had a set of steps to get into the lorry tray. The twins were taken to the back seat of a rather large car. This was their third ride in a car but it was not the car that was memorable this time but everything happening around the car. There were people, donkeys, carts and even a couple of camels crossing their paths; the driver was continually honking his horn. There seemed to be no women, only men in the streets. The noise, even without the car horn, was deafening and the smell was not too pleasant.

Finally, after about an hour of very slow-moving traffic, they arrived at the gates of a very large and impressive building. These gates were being guarded by a troop of soldiers who shooed the crowd away to allow the two vehicles entry. Once inside the courtyard, they could see two flights of steps leading to the main entrance. They both commented that this was not the ideal entrance for a hospital. This was because the building had been a large hotel that had been commandeered by the army and then converted into a hospital. They climbed the stairs and were escorted to the matron's office. Most of the matrons they had met were middle-aged or elderly women; this one looked not much older than the twins.

The matron looked up as the twins entered.

"I was told I was getting twins but I did not know you would be identical. At present, we have two wards, one for the officers and one for the soldiers. You will each run one ward. I want a report from both wards every day. I will call a sister who will show you your quarters and the wards."

"Thank you, matron. We are here to do our best and we know that as the war picks up, we will have more patients."

The matron was in shock but was saved from responding because a sister came and told her to show the ladies to their quarters and wards. The sister ushered them towards their quarters but the twins wanted to go to the wards. Again, there was a moment of silence and a sister rooted to the spot. This lady was used to shocks and she reacted quickly. As they entered the officer's ward, there was silence and after the twins spoke together, there was more silence.

"One of us will be in charge of this ward and the other will be in charge of the soldier's ward. Our names are Agnes and Elizabeth and we will be back shortly, so do not go away."

As they left the ward, they heard one officer laugh, followed by the rest. The sister found her voice: "Some of the soldiers use bad language and there are a couple of Australians who are particularly bad."

"That will be no problem for us; our father says that soldiers seem to moderate their language when we are around."

They entered the next ward and silence once again descended.

"We have just arrived and one of us will be in charge of this ward. We will come later and talk to each patient but for now we need a bath and some lunch. We notice there are some empty beds; we assume you are expecting visitors."

With that, they left the ward and could hear one soldier shouting, "Visitors!" and the whole ward erupted in laughter.

The sister showed them to their quarters; it was a large room with two beds (bigger than a normal single), a table and chairs, a wardrobe, a chest of drawers, a washbasin and a jug. The sister said there were showers that the army had rigged; the problem was that they were communal. As the twins had seniority, they could pick their times. The matron had a bath and never used the showers. The army wanted the nurses not to use too much water, so they discouraged using baths.

"We have no problem with sharing showers; we are country girls."

"The showers are often cold, as the army is having difficulty with the boilers. Some idiot army man told all the Egyptian staff they were no longer needed. Of course, the boilers broke down along with other equipment and the officers in charge appear to be too stubborn to call some of the Egyptian staff back."

"Again, cold water is no problem for us."

The first shower was cold and the twins thought they had spoken too hastily. At lunch, all the nurses were silent, so the twins thought that they would have to ignore the effect of their speech and introduce themselves. That broke the ice and then the complaints flowed freely and strongly. Most were about the matron, who seemed to have eyes everywhere but rarely left her office. After lunch, the twins descended on the officer's ward. In the manner of the old saying, 'The silence was deafening,' so they went first to the bedridden officers, both with abdominal wounds. They examined the wounds while the others watched. The twins explained they had an uncle with a similar wound and he had lost his shyness when they nursed him. Finally, one officer asked how he could tell the twins apart. The twins pointed to the small medal and said in unison, "Agnes" and then pointed to the uniform with no medal and said

"Elizabeth." Now the officers were smiling and gently laughing.

After this, the twins entered the soldiers' ward and asked the sister to point out the two Australian soldiers. One was bedridden\ and the other had lost most of his left leg and was sitting by his mate's bed. The twins went to them and said, "We have never been to Australia but our uncle told us a lot about it. We understand the centre is desert and most of the population lives around the coast."

The two soldiers were silent.

"Don't be afraid; now where are you from?"

Finally, the bedridden patient said, "Ballarat."

"That's in Victoria and they have gold mines. Where are you from?" turning to the other soldier.

"I'm from Sydney, ladies."

"That is supposed to have the most beautiful harbour in the world."

"It sure does."

Now both the Australian soldiers were talking and all the other soldiers were listening. The twins went to all the other soldiers and told them what they knew about their hometowns. One Scotsman was from Glasgow, so they told him they had visited the infirmary and hoped he would see that place and be home in the near future. They added that he should not spend too long in the hospital, as his relatives might want him home. As they left the ward, everyone was smiling. They had seen an office at the far end of the ward and would investigate that the next day. They wrote a brief report in which they said that they had decided that Agnes would look after the officer's ward and Elizabeth the Soldier's Ward and they hoped that would be suitable for the matron. Dinner was less quiet and the cold shower had them ready for bed. They were up early the next morning so they could meet the night shift nurses. These nurses appeared to have no complaints but then again, they were probably in shock at the unison speech.

Now to work, all the officers had wheelchairs allocated, even the bedridden officers. Agnes wheeled some on to the balcony to get fresh air. The soldiers also had a balcony but there were only four wheelchairs, so Elizabeth arranged two seats to enable six men to sit on the balcony. She apologised to the bedridden soldiers but promised they would think of something to improve this situation. The soldiers were amazed that they were getting apologies; this was well outside of their normal army experience.

The twins decided to investigate the office at the end of the soldiers' ward and there they found a captain, with half of his leg removed, sitting at a desk. He had watched the twins in the ward and so showed no surprise when they spoke to him. They asked how he had lost his leg. He told them he was told he had been hit by a mortar shell, as he had passed out when his leg was hit and had no memory of the event after the explosion. The army wanted to send him back to England but he declined; he wanted to do something useful here. He kept records of all the patients and was expecting to get busy soon. His records also had items such as drugs and bandages; he even had inventories of the disinfectant used. He was like a quartermaster. The captain was from Coventry and they had a talk about the Midlands. The twins asked where he slept and he told them he had a separate room, that with his wheelchair and crutches he could get around the hospital. That would get easier when his wooden leg was fitted; it was currently being made by the engineering corps.

The twins enjoyed that interlude with the captain and decided they would help him when his wooden leg appeared. In the afternoon, they were together in the soldier's ward when the surgeon, with the rank of major, visited the captain's office. The captain had warned the major about the two new senior sisters and so when he met them and they spoke, he only had a limited shock. They took the major to meet all the soldiers and then to the other ward to meet the officers. When they were finished, he took them on one side and told them the Turks were making a push for the Suez Canal and there might be a flood of casualties in the next few days. He warned them that was secret information and he was telling them because he believed the matron was 'in another world'.

"Tomorrow I am going to relax and ride out to the pyramids. I think I will not have more time until we get another surgeon or two."

"We ride, sir."

"Do you ride side-saddle?"

"No, sir, we have split skirts and ride as well as many men, even if we say so ourselves."

"If you would like to ride tomorrow, meet me at the stable at six fifteen in the morning."

"We know where the stables are, as we have already talked to the horses."

"You talk to horses? I have to see this."

The next morning, the major arrived at the stable to see the twins talking to two horses. He watched for a few minutes and then approached them.

"I see you have picked out your two horses; they look like good mounts."

"Yes, these horses seem to like us and listen to what we say."

"Do you want the grooms to saddle them?"

"No, thank you, sir; we will do that."

The twins saddled the horses and mounted them. The horses stood still during this process. The major's horse had to be held by the groom so he could mount. Even then, the horse moved as if in protest and the major was thinking the twins had put a spell on their horses. They walked the horses out of the stable to be met by an armed soldier with a rifle on his back, who saluted them and the major. The twins just nodded, not wanting to scare the soldier.

"I always take an armed guard just in case of trouble, although I don't expect anything this early in the morning."

They rode at a trot, then at a canter and finally at a gallop. The twins were riding in front and the soldier told the major that these ladies could really ride. There were very few people or animals around and when they neared the pyramids, they were completely alone. The twins stopped very close to the first pyramid. They turned and said in unison to the major that the wind was making strange sounds. The guard sat upright and could only stare at the twins.

"Yes, I find that sound soothing and it makes me feel at peace."

They galloped to the next pyramid and the twins told the major that the sound was there but slightly different.

The major listened and said, "I have never really noticed that; maybe your four ears are better than my two."

Now they were all laughing, including the soldier.

"I think we should be getting back for breakfast, as I am hungry."

The twins agreed and took off at a gallop. The soldier was quick to tell the major he was available for a ride at any time, especially with these young ladies. The twins were early for breakfast as they were feeling hungry; the ride had given them an appetite. The twins hurried back to their wards, as they knew there were casualties coming to the hospital. There were indeed two officers and a dozen soldiers just arriving. Actually, the soldier's ward only had ten spare beds, so they sent the nurses looking for additional beds.

There was a flurry of activity and in a moment of calm, one of the officers already in the ward said that perhaps both twins should greet the new officers. He had been told one was a major who would outrank the other officers in the ward and would expect to be treated accordingly. The twins realised what was happening, so they went along with the joke. The two new officers were wheeled in and the twins welcomed them. Of course, both were in shock and there was silence until the twins left the ward. In the soldier's ward, the new patients were all in one area and as the twins entered, it all went quiet. The twins introduced themselves and there were a dozen faces just staring at them. One of the old patients shouted across that these two sisters were scarier than the enemy and the new lads should behave themselves. The frozen moment passed and there was loud laughter.

After that bit of fun, Agnes went back to the officer's ward and Elizabeth went to talk to the captain, John, in his temporary office. He told her there were four Australians in this bunch and most of the incoming casualties had leg wounds but two had abdominal injuries and as such, would be bedridden. The surgeon came and asked Elizabeth to accompany him as he examined the new arrivals. He had already seen and talked to the two officers in Agnes's ward. He examined the wounds of the enlisted men and commented that the cleansing and binding of most of them had been well done in the field hospitals but he confided in Elizabeth that one man might have an infection; he would take him the next day for a better look.

After the surgeon had left, Elizabeth went to talk to each new patient. One surprised her. He said he had been bought in on the back of a lorry with a black soldier. When the stretcher bearers came for them, he went one way and the black soldier went another way. He asked the bearers about this, who said the black soldier was going to his own ward. This soldier noticed there were no black soldiers in this ward. Elizabeth listened quietly and after talking to the soldier, went to talk to John. He knew nothing about a ward for black soldiers but had wondered why they did not have any black patients. He thought they may have been taken to a different hospital. Agnes appeared at that point, as she knew what they were talking about. The soldier had told Elizabeth that he was taken to the left and the black soldier had been taken to the right, towards the back of the hospital. The twins thought they would have a quick lunch and investigate. They had never been to the back of the hospital. A stroll on the grounds might be interesting.

They walked slowly towards the rear and saw an armed guard in front of two large doors. They approached him and mentally decided just one of them should speak. He seemed to be half asleep but the sight of two identical ladies soon had him awake. They asked what was behind the doors and he told them he thought it was a ward but he had never been inside. They then spoke in unison and said that was what they were looking for. The sentry was dumbstruck and allowed them to pass and open the doors. He said to himself that he had never heard the like; it was unbelievable.

The smell hit them; it was a mixture of urine and wounds (it brought back memories of the estate). They entered a large, poorly lit room with no windows and obviously little ventilation. There was a slope down, so the room was partly below ground level. As their eyes adjusted to the gloom, they saw some soldiers seated around a table and some lying on beds. They spotted a nurse, approached her and again decided only one would speak. All the time, they could not believe what they were seeing.

Agnes asked, "Do you speak English?"

"Yes, ma'am, I went to an English school in Kenya."

"How many patients do you have and how many nurses?

"We are four nurses, two on day shift and two on night shift. At present, we have ten soldiers; we have been here for a month and two of the soldiers arrived yesterday."

"Does a doctor visit these patents?"

"We have an Egyptian doctor come in once a week."

"Do you have any Zulus?"

"There is one man and the rest are from different parts of Africa."

The other nurse wandered over and listened to the conversation. The twins decided to speak in unison: "We are nurses from the floor above you and we have come to try to get you a better ward. I am nurse Agnes and I am nurse Elizabeth."

The whole ward was silent and the nurses stood back, open-mouthed.

"We understand that one soldier is a Zulu and to him we say "Sawabona" (greetings), the only word we know in the Zulu language. To the rest of you, we say greetings."

Not one soldier moved, so the twins took the nurse and went to see each soldier to understand their wounds.

These soldiers shook their heads and nodded but no one spoke. The twins left, telling the nurse they would try to come back tomorrow and bring wheel chairs to get some of the soldiers out into the sunlight. They also complimented the nurses on the way the patients were bandaged.

Outside, they were almost in tears; that was a shocking place. They had seen some poor hospitals in their time but never a ward like that one. As they walked back to their wards, they decided on a strategy. The next morning, they went to see the matron and asked whether they could borrow a couple of wheelchairs to take the black soldiers into the sunlight.

"We have no spare wheelchairs, so go back to your duties."

The twins left the office without saying a word, although they were surprised. They went straight to Captain John and told him about this so-called ward. He told them he had to see this for himself. They offered to push his wheelchair but he said he would use his crutches, as he needed practice before he received his wooden leg. Elizabeth guided him towards the black soldiers and left to go back to her ward. The sentry saluted as Captain John passed; he was in full uniform, including his cap. As John opened the doors, he stood back to allow the stale air to escape. He had been brought up on a farm but found this odour offensive coming from a hospital ward.

John stepped slowly inside and carefully descended the slope. He was greeted by one of the nurses. He told her he was going to get information from the patients and the nurses. His notebook was full before he left and he told the nurses to shut the doors later. He also instructed the sentry to help the nurses when they shut the doors. As he walked back, he was shaking. John was really angry and when he reached his office, he called Elizabeth.

"I can hardly believe that hellhole exists in this hospital."

The Black Hole of Calcutta was embedded in British Army folklore.

Elizabeth said that she and Agnes were going to take two wheelchairs and get some of the soldiers into the sunlight. She asked whether they could borrow his wheelchair.

"Of course, you can; put it to better use than sitting in my office. We have a new administrator and I will let him know about that abominable ward. I have no record of it and I don't know how they get their supplies."

Agnes approached one of the bedridden officers and asked if she could borrow his wheelchair.

"Take the bloody thing; it is no use to me. I am sorry for swearing but the army frustrates me sometimes and I want to go home soon. I am lying here in bed with a wheelchair I can't use and no information about my future posting."

"I understand and I don't want to get your hopes up but I hear there is a hospital ship coming to Alexandria. Please, do not repeat that, as it is only a rumour so far."

After a quick lunch, the twins took the wheelchairs to the black soldiers' ward. Agnes left Elizabeth with the nurses and went back to the wards to cover for her. That was no problem because she removed her medal when she went to the soldier's ward. The sisters in each ward did not notice the deception. Agnes was smiling at this because she knew that, back at home, Benjamin would have noticed immediately. Elizabeth helped the nurses get six soldiers into the sunlight. She apologised to the soldiers for not being able to leave the ward and said they would try to get them all out of the ward soon. Not one soldier spoke to her. Elizabeth went back to her room and went straight to see John.

"I was just talking to you; how come you are back so soon?"

"You were talking to Agnes and through my link to her, I know what you were saying. She has been covering for me."

"Gadzooks, you two are unbelievable."

After a couple of hours, Agnes left her medal with Elizabeth and went to help take the soldiers inside and bring the wheelchairs back to their owners. At dinner, the twins were pleased with themselves but they would have a shock in the morning. After breakfast, they were called to the matron's office.

"You disobeyed my orders and took two wheelchairs to be used by ordinary soldiers. There will be a disciplinary hearing at two o'clock this afternoon. You are in the army and have disobeyed a senior officer."

The twins did not speak and left the matron's office. The matron obviously had spies and had set up this hearing at breakneck speed. Now they wanted some information from John. Bertie had told them about civil courts but what about a military court?

"Normally, there will be three senior officers and someone taking notes. The most senior officer will read out the charge and then ask for your statement. The matron may be there but she does not have to attend. If you want to call me, I will testify that you had my permission to use my chair."

"We don't think that will be necessary and now we have to plan our strategy."

As they left his office, John was smiling at the idea of the twins planning strategy. These ladies had him in love.

Uncle Bertie had told them about trials and his first advice was to listen to the charge and the evidence before saying anything. They should take particular note of the wording of the charge. They should never call anyone a liar, although they could infer that someone was not telling the truth. Do not interrupt the judge or magistrate. With these instructions in mind, they thought that they would beat the charge and decided that, of course, they were going to speak in unison. They were going to give this panel of officers a big shock.

They were ushered into a room with three officers facing them. The one in the middle was a colonel, who turned out to be the new administrator. They were expecting a general but thought that this would be a good test to see what type of man he was. To his right was an Australian Major and to his left was another major, their surgeon. There was a corporal to take notes.

The colonel said this was not a serious charge but the matron had said they took wheelchairs from the ward after she had clearly ordered them not to take the chairs. The matron was not present and now the twins had to tell their side of the story.

Now the twins spoke in unison: "We asked the matron if we could borrow spare wheelchairs to take black soldiers into the sunlight. She told us there were no spare chairs but gave no order. She just told us to resume our duties."

The colonel sat back in his chair and could only stare at the twins. The Australian major did likewise; the surgeon had his hand over his mouth to stop himself from laughing.

"We found a ward below ground having ten injured black soldiers and two nurses. The ward was a large windowless room with poor ventilation."

The twins refrained from talking about the smell.

"This was a very unsanitary ward and we had permission from two officers to use their wheelchairs. We took six of the black soldiers into the sunlight for two hours and apologised to the other four soldiers."

The colonel and the major were still in shock but the surgeon was interested in what the twins had to say.

"We are here as nurses to help injured soldiers, no matter what their rank, or nationality, or colour and we were doing our duty."

The twins stopped talking and the colonel found his voice.

"I have only been here four days but I know nothing of the ward."

The surgeon spoke up. "I have been here for over a month and have never heard of or seen this ward."

"Ladies, can I ask you to step outside for a few minutes? I need to consult with my colleagues."

As they were leaving the ward, they noticed the corporal beaming like a Cheshire cat. Within a few minutes, they were called back into the office.

"I am very sorry; this was an ill-conceived charge but it has brought to our attention important information and we thank you for that. There will be nothing on your record but there will be an investigation of the so-called ward."

"Thank you, sir and now that we know you are the new administrator, we would like to ask for your indulgence in regard to another matter."

The colonel was still taken aback by their speech and wanted to hear more of it, so he was never going to deny them talking to him.

"We are getting bedridden patients, generally with abdominal wounds. It is difficult to take them out into the sunlight. Our uncle is a major who was wounded in the Boer War. His abdominal wound meant that he was totally bedridden. We designed a wheelchair so that we could slide him off his bed; then the wheelchair adjusted into a more normal configuration. The benefit was that he could see around him in a normal manner and he learned to use the chair to get around. Do you think we could find the facilities here to build such a chair?"

"Well, we have a corps of engineers and I will get someone to talk to you. Thank you for bringing this to my attention."

The twins left the room and the officers went into a huddle. The colonel was livid that no one had told him about the underground ward. The surgeon had to see this ward and the Australian officer was marvelling at two ladies designing a wheelchair.

The twins went back to their wards, glad that the hearing had backfired on the matron. Agnes was soon confronted by the surgeon, who wanted her to take him to this ward. He told her they should go at once and tell her sister they would be back within the hour. As they approached the sentry, he stood at attention but said he had orders that no one should enter that ward. The major took off his white medical coat to show his rank.

"Whoever gave you those orders probably should be locked up but I am countermanding those orders; open those doors."

Agnes said she had forgotten to warn him of the smell, which hit him as soon as the doors opened.

"Nurse, if you want to leave, I will understand."

"No, sir, you forget I have been here several times."

The major greeted the black nurses and took one with him to talk to each patient; at least the patients were talking to him. Agnes talked to the other nurse, whose English was not so good. She told Agnes that the soldiers were afraid of the twins because they were not normal. Agnes had to laugh at that phrase. As Agnes and the major walked back to the front of the hospital, he said he was very angry. He could not understand how he had been in the hospital for over a month and knew nothing of this monstrosity.

"How could this happen? I have been here for over a month and it was kept secret. If news of this ward were to leak to the press and then the public, the army would get a black eye; no pun intended. After I examined the soldiers, I suspect that one soldier may have gangrene setting in on his stump. I will take an orderly and bring him to the main hospital so I can examine his wound. I can't thank you enough for bringing this abomination to our attention. I am going to recommend one of those nurses be promoted to sister. I am not going to talk to the matron right now, as I might lose my temper."

Elizabeth had been talking to John, telling him about the proceedings. He decided to investigate the first floor to see if there was any suitable room for a new ward. Elizabeth told him that they had never investigated the other floors but a definite problem was the stairs.

Back in the ward, the surgeon consulted John. John told him he had found a large room on the same floor that could be used as a ward. The surgeon offered to push him there in his wheelchair but John said he wanted to use his crutches.

"Yes, I must inquire about what happened to your wooden leg. I think we could have bought one in the local market; it would have been quicker." They both laughed as they went off.

Meanwhile, a nurse reported to Agnes that a colonel had gone to the matron's office and was heard shouting something like "Why have I not been told?" Agnes smiled and told the nurse not to repeat this, as the colonel was the new administrator.

The surgeon and John returned to John's office to be joined by the colonel. He wanted to see the black soldier's ward and the potential new ward. John showed him the list of black patients and their injuries. John also warned the colonel of the offensive odour that he was about to experience.

"I have been around stables all my life; I was in the cavalry."

The surgeon said, "When you are less busy, you should ride out to the pyramids with the twins. These ladies ride like men and are as good as most men."

"Is there nothing these twins cannot do?"

The surgeon and colonel went off to visit the black soldier's ward. John was smiling at that last remark and he wished he could ride to the pyramids with the twins. Elizabeth and Agnes were investigating the second and third floors of the former hotel. One problem was that the lift was not working. After the exodus of the Egyptian workers, it had broken down. There were many rooms on the two upper floors for wards but none were suitable for disabled soldiers. The twins decided to talk to the colonel about bringing some Egyptian workers back. They had no chance for a while, as the colonel was so incensed at the situation that he wanted the soldiers to move out immediately, even if only under canvas in the courtyard.

John advised the colonel that the army camp next door had plenty of manpower. The colonel set about visiting the army camp located just outside the hospital boundary. The surgeon needed some wheelchairs and John offered his chair. The surgeon said he would visit the store and see what was held there and when he came back, he was absolutely fuming; he had found that there were several unused chairs in the store. He asked Agnes whether he could borrow her ward sister and one of the nurses to get at least one black soldier out of that ward. Agnes told him the only thing she wanted him to do was to warn the nurses about the smell. As he walked away, he was laughing to himself; these twins always thought of others.

The matron was sitting in her office alone, deep in silent thought. She had been bypassed by the actions going on. She knew her days were numbered.

There was a hive of activity that swept the hospital as the colonel came back with a large group of soldiers. They were going to push wheelchairs and beds to the new ward on the first floor. The colonel appointed the twins to be jointly in charge of the new ward and he promoted one of the black nurses to sister. He did not bother to inform the matron of the changes. Now he started to look at the rooms and their future potential across the whole building.

The twins met him on the stairs between the second and third floors. They told him there were many rooms suitable for wounded soldiers; the only problem was the broken lift. They asked the colonel whether he could get some of the old Egyptian staff to run the lift. On his way to his office, he was asking himself whether he should simply let the twins take charge of the hospital and just sit in his office and relax as some sort of figurehead.

The black sister told the twins that the soldiers were very happy with their new ward. It was all happening so fast that they had to get their bearings and then take the time to carefully tell the patients what was going to happen to them, so they were not confused.

"They don't seem to talk to us; why?"

"First of all, when they see you together, these soldiers think they are seeing double. They close one eye and there are still two of you. I have seen twins but never identical twins and none of the soldiers have ever seen identical twins. Then, when you speak, they can't tell who is talking. In many African languages, one person speaks directly to another person. Tonal languages require the listener to understand the tone and facial expressions to get the meaning of what is being said. Even if these soldiers understand English, which is hard for them anyway. They are too absorbed in looking at you, so they cannot reply."

"Nurse, you have just taught us many things we did not know. We will have to go away and digest this new knowledge."

John was often in the black soldier's ward; he was generally accompanying Elizabeth. The soldiers would talk to him but were afraid to talk to Elizabeth. The officers in Agnes's ward had heard about the new ward and one captain had previously served in Khartoum. The British army had been training Sudanese soldiers since the relief of Khartoum by Kitchener. This officer knew some Arabic and asked Agnes whether he could meet these soldiers. Agnes had thought that most officers were generally not interested in the welfare of ordinary soldiers; this was definitely a step for the better, so she could not deny this request.

The move of the black soldiers had gone very well and the black nurses were given a large room for their accommodation. At last, they could move out of the tent into the army compound. John was liaising with them as he was in charge of the distribution of bandages, drugs and other items needed in the ward. He was reporting to Elizabeth that these were very efficient nurses. The colonel had visited the ward and was very pleased. He told the twins that they were getting additional help from a surgeon and three doctors, including an Indian doctor who specialised in tropical medicine. The hospital would have a new ward for sick soldiers with malaria, typhoid or cholera. There would also be a venereal disease ward staffed by male nurses.

"Yes, colonel, we have seen such wards in Britain."

"I regard catching a venereal disease as self-inflicted and I have no time for those soldiers. If cured, they can go back to the front. Unfortunately, we have to house them in this hospital; at least they can be on the second floor. I have the intelligence corps looking to get some Egyptians back to operate some of the facilities. Thank you for the suggestion; it is a good one but I think it will take time."

One day, Elizabeth was entertaining the Australian troops and they were laughing. A sergeant from their brigade had come to visit and he stood in the background listening to laughing wounded soldiers. One of the sisters took him and introduced him to Elizabeth.

"I am sure these soldiers would like to talk to you rather than me."

One soldier said, "We are not sure about that." Everyone laughed, including the sergeant.

When Elizabeth retreated, the sister asked why she spent time with the Australian soldiers in particular.

"When we came here, we were told the Australian patients could be difficult and use bad language. My sister and I decided to shock them by speaking in unison. Then we talked about Australia and we had a very quiet bunch of soldiers. I try to cheer them up every day. They are a long way from home and talking about their home helps them."

Within two days, an Australian officer appeared and asked for Sister Elizabeth.

"Good morning, sir; your soldiers are over there."

"Before I see my soldiers, I want to know how you make wounded men laugh."

Agnes joined them and they said in unison, "We first put them in shock."

The officer stood still and after a short time, said, "That worked on me."

Agnes excused herself and Elizabeth explained to him that they first talked about Australia.

"These men are a long way from home and want to go home as soon as possible. They are also worried about what awaits them when they get home, because they are not the same in body or mind as when they left."

"They are not the only ones."

"I come from the country and most of these men are from the bush. I talk about my ability to talk to animals. We did not have sheep but if I want them to laugh, I only have to start telling them about talking to pigs and goats. These are the most difficult animals to converse with, so I tell them to try talking to sheep as a start when they get home."

"If these soldiers start to talk to sheep, men in white coats will come and take them away."

"I tell them to do it quietly; I know some people may not understand."

The officer was laughing and some of the men recognised him. "Well, talking to animals has me almost as much in shock as you and your sister speaking in unison. By the way, did your sister join us by accident?"

"No, sir, she knew what we were talking about."

"But she was in the other room."

"Yes, sir, we communicate by thought."

"I don't believe in magic but you have given me food for thought. Well, I think I might have nightmares tonight and they will have nothing to do with the enemy or combat. I have come to give these soldiers a promise that we will get them home soon."

"That will be just the news they are awaiting. I understand they are volunteers and many are married, so going home is always on their mind."

"I only hope their wives and families can cope."

Later on, the soldiers were excitedly telling Elizabeth that the officer had said there was a ship coming to Suez. It was a converted liner able to transport both soldiers and horses. That ship was going to transport them to Australia. They also told Elizabeth that there would be replacements and that Elizabeth should try her magic on them. Elizabeth told them she would give them a shock and entertain them. These were now a much happier bunch of soldiers but they were also aware that there were always casualties in war and that there would be new chums occupying these same beds soon enough. They were hoping their replacements in the ward would enjoy these nurses and their antics.

In the meantime, a lieutenant and a sergeant from the engineering corps came to talk to the twins. The initial shock was less for the sergeant, who had been warned by one of the guards. The lieutenant just stood opened, looking at the twins.

"We are in luck; one of our men was apprenticed to a carriage maker. We borrowed a wheelchair and took a good look at it. Our unit is used to building bigger structures like bridges and ramps, so this will be a new challenge."

The twins took a wheelchair and put it beside a bed. With the large wheel touching the bed, there would be a gap, so they explained that there had to be a way of sliding the tray to be flush with the bed. Also, as the seat was taken up with the footrest, the front had to be stabilised. The twins had a drawing of the design needed and the sergeant busied himself with taking measurements. The lieutenant was still just staring at the twins. The sergeant promised to be back in a few days when they had a prototype. The twins told him they would try it out on an officer, which had the sergeant in fits of laughter. The officer continued watching without saying a word; he appeared to be completely in awe of the twins.

Now there was intake and discharge movement in and out of the wards on a regular basis, except for the black soldier ward. The officer who had been in Khartoum said he would try to find a rich Sudanese in Cairo and see if they could somehow get some soldiers back to Khartoum. The twins had found some small carriages in the back of the stables. These sulkies could be used to take wounded soldiers to see the pyramids and also to take the officer into Cairo to find these Sudanese. The colonel was also trying to see if he could find ships that would be calling into Kenyan ports. Transporting the Nigerian and Gold Coast soldiers was a more difficult problem again and would need further investigation and thought.

The twins were writing one or two letters a week to their father and Bertie. They were also writing to Alice's brother, whom they always called the Major. They also composed a special letter written to Benjamin describing the hospital and the desert around the hospital; they included some sketched images of the hospital and the pyramids. Writing letters took little time but gave the twins lots of pleasure. They thought that they might practise their drawing if they could find the time, as it may help Bertie and Benjamin 'see their world'. Bertie loved these letters full of information about Egypt. He vowed to take Elsie and Benjamin to Cairo when the war ended. The twins were always writing that they missed Arthur and Benjamin. Because of this, Bertie's letters often started with the development of the two boys; they were both growing and Bertie thought they would eventually be as tall as Reggie, who was considered a tall man in their district. Each letter normally contained a few paragraphs from Reggie. These were mainly about the estate and how well it was doing. To their surprise and pleasure, he wrote that their grandmother had visited recently and actually asked about the twins. Reggie did not write about the dreadful news of the war in Europe (the twins were getting plenty of news through the army, censored, of course). Alice wrote about Arthur and her parents. She also commented that she thought Reggie was drinking too much cider (not to tell Reggie). Elsie's sister was enjoying living in Birmingham and might be expecting a second child. The twins started to ask themselves whether they would ever have children. They would love to have a child like their cousin Benjamin.

The major wrote long letters, as he was now managing his father's estate. He was talking to the horses and they seemed to respond. He said that he would definitely not talk to the pigs. His mother suspected his father was talking to the chickens. The milk yield was good as the milk maid talked to the dairy cows. The best news was about his wheelchair. A harness had been fitted so that the chair could be pulled by a small horse. The major was now able to visit Alice's house and the local pub. All the drinkers would come outside to talk to him. The only problem was that he wondered if he was interesting in his own right, because he had noticed that they always wanted to talk about the twins. A bit of secret news was that he was going to propose to his nurse when he had summoned up the courage. She was a widow of similar age and she would pull him off the bed onto the wheelchair and vice versa without help. His legs were still useless but he had gained much upper-body strength, so he could help a bit. He had no secrets from her and she was very efficient while also being kind to him. The twins loved his letters and were excited about the prospect of a coming marriage. They had visions of their uncle being dragged into his chair. If he did get married, his nurse could be an ideal wife.

Agnes asked Elizabeth whether they should swap wards but Elizabeth told her she wanted to stay near John. Agnes realised at that point that Elizabeth was sweet on John. They were now watching as the matron was packing her belongings. She was being transferred to a field hospital. The new matron was an Australian and they expected her to arrive at any time. A couple of the Australian soldiers told Elizabeth that this could well be a 'tough old bird'.

One day before the matron was due to arrive, a handsome new officer came into Elizabeth's ward, asking for directions to the matron's office.

"You are not British and your Australian accent is different" commented Elizabeth.

"No, I am from New Zealand; I am the new surgeon."

"You look very young, if you don't mind me saying so."

"I am not that young and this is indeed my first posting but I have seen enough to know that it is the matron who runs any hospital."

"We are just getting a new matron and if you go through the next ward, they will direct you to the senior surgeon's office."

"Thank you, sister; you are the first person to give me any information."

The captain strolled into the next ward and stopped in his tracks. Standing in front of him was Agnes.

"How did you get here before me? I just left you in that other ward."

'You met my sister; we are identical twins. I will tell her to come so that you can see for yourself."

Agnes looked towards the ward, said nothing and Elizabeth soon came through the door.

"How did you do that?"

The twins then spoke in unison, "We know what the other twin is thinking and saying, even if we are separated."

The captain stood still and then, after a while, said, "Well, er, well."

Agnes spoke to the captain while Elizabeth went back to her ward. "Your reaction was normal; we generally use it for shock value. I am Agnes and wear a small medal on my tunic; my sister is Elizabeth. I understand you want to see the matron but she is not here, so I will take you to the surgeon. He is an easy-going man and I am sure you will get along."

All the captain could do was nod in the affirmative. Agnes knocked on the door and they entered to see the major sitting at his desk.

"Douglas, I see you have met the twins and are probably still in shock. Don't worry; even I was in shock at our first meeting. Thank you, Agnes; we will visit your ward a little later."

Agnes left the room and now she knew the new captain's name, as did Elizabeth. Douglas was offered a seat and the major asked about his education and experience.

"I come from the South Island from a farming family of Scottish descent. I did my medical studies at the University of Otago. There was a medical facility there that trained military medical personnel. I have interned at a few hospitals but this is my first surgical appointment."

"Don't worry none of your past experiences will be like what you will experience here. This is a large hospital and we get wounded soldiers in from the front. Most will have already been patched up in a field hospital and we will generally only receive the difficult cases. Occasionally, we will get injured soldiers from places where we are the nearest hospital but as the war moves eastwards, we will see very few of them in the future. We examine the wounds of every patient as they come in, particularly looking for infection, gangrene or botched surgery. Most field hospitals do a good job but confidentially, I think they do too many amputations. At present, we do very few. Now, I will see you tomorrow at eight a.m. outside the operating theatre."

Douglas went back to Agnes's ward, ostensibly to see the officers convalescing but really to take a better look at Agnes. She greeted him and introduced him to the officers in her ward. Only a couple of the officers were younger than Douglas and there were no New Zealanders. There were two Australians but Douglas had only visited Perth on the liner that brought him to Egypt, so they had little in common. Agnes sat him down at her desk and asked if he would like to visit the black soldier's ward.

"I understand you have Māori tribes in New Zealand but these are black African soldiers. They won't talk to me or my sister, as apparently, we put the fear of god or maybe gods into them." Agnes was laughing at this thought and Douglas thought that he loved her laugh.

"Yes, I want to see all the patients in this hospital. This is my first surgical posting and I want to learn as I go."

"I can show you most of the hospital but I cannot take you to the Venereal Disease Ward," Agnes was laughing again. Douglas loved that laugh; it seemed so soothing in a difficult environment.

They went to the soldier's ward, where they met Elizabeth again and Douglas was introduced to Captain John. Douglas then met most of the soldiers but found that not one of them was a New Zealander. The Australian soldiers told him they adored the twins, as they were the only ones in this place who could make them laugh. Entering the black soldier's ward, the sister on duty stood at attention and then shook Douglas's hand when he offered it. The sister took him to meet the troops while Agnes stood in the background talking to the other nurse.

Douglas was very interested in this ward and the soldiers. "When this war has ended, I want to see more of Africa. A lot of our school stories were about wild animals and they were mostly about Africa. I have not seen England yet; actually, I have basically seen nothing of the world."

"I think you might like the countryside in England; do you ride?"

"Yes, I was brought up on a large farm and we had plenty of sheep. Riding and shooting feral animals was my sport; I never played much rugby. We had dogs to round up the sheep but we often had a ride to find them all. If I close my eyes, I can see our farm and those sheep. What I have seen of Egypt so far is very different from back home."

Douglas had a satisfied look on his face, which Agnes was closely studying. She took him back to the major's office and told Douglas she would see him later.

"Well, sir, Sister Agnes has shown me the wards on this floor and I am pleasantly surprised. I had visions of a quiet hospital with angry soldiers wanting to go home. I am sure they all want to go home but they seem to be making the best of the situation. The wards I just saw were cleaner than the ones back home. I am impressed."

"Yes, without the twins, this would be a different hospital. When you go to the wards on the upper floor, you will see a different standard because the twins don't go there. I think we should join the nurses for lunch. I do so when I am feeling a bit down because they cheer me up. It will be a good chance for you to be introduced to the other nurses."

The lunchroom was a chatty place but went silent when the surgeons walked in through the double doors.

"Please, don't stop talking; we are here so I can introduce Captain Douglas, our new surgeon, who has come all the way from New Zealand. He will be around the wards a lot and he does not know it yet but he will also be doing some night duties and will meet the night nurses."

Two chairs were made available opposite the twins. Douglas was now wondering what would happen next.

"Please, Agnes and Elizabeth, do not talk in unison; you will put Douglas right off his lunch."

Then all the nurses started to laugh. The twins stayed silent and were smiling. They pointed to the black sister sitting next to Elizabeth, indicating she should speak.

"I am a nurse, Njoki, when I first saw these senior sisters looking the same, I was in shock and when they spoke together, the shock got worse. Of course, I soon adjusted to them but my patients just cannot adjust. They can't talk to the sisters at all but they cannot stop talking about them. I have to ask the sisters to come one by one to our ward; otherwise, our patients will become incoherent. So, sir, you are not alone in preferring to see them one at a time."

The whole table was in an uproar after this speech and even Douglas was laughing. This was such an enjoyable lunch that the major said they should do it at least once a week. The major told Douglas that now it was time to look at the other wards and talk to the other doctors. He told him in particular to talk to the Indian doctor, who was a very interesting person.

The next day, Douglas was called to a meeting to be introduced to the colonel. This was a meeting of all the doctors and senior staff, including the twins. The colonel was in a very good mood. Supplies had been dwindling, particularly from Britain. The war in Europe was going very badly and vast quantities of supplies were needed in France. However, things should get better soon, as new supplies are coming from Australia, India and South

Africa. These will be further supplemented by supplies from America. His other news was that the Empire forces were pushing the Turks and their allies back. Those included Germans and that pleased the colonel. Further news was that the new matron had arrived in the country from Australia and they would welcome her soon. He told them that some of the Egyptian staff were coming back to the hospital and as a result, hopefully the lift and boilers would soon be working normally.

Afterwards, Douglas met the colonel, who confided that he assumed the twins had baffled Douglas as much as he had been at their first meeting. He said they were instrumental in a lot of jolly good things around the hospital but not to worry; in the typical army way, he was going to claim the credit. They both laughed. The colonel was keen to get many of the soldiers' home and said that the ship that came from Australia was going to dock at Mombasa on the way back and so several of the black soldiers would be able to get home. One of the injured officers had met some Sudanese in Cairo and the Sudanese soldiers would be put on a boat down the Nile. At the border, they would be transferred to another boat and taken to Atbara. There was an army camp in Atbara and from there, they would be sent to Khartoum by train. The Colonel said that this had taken an enormous amount of organisation and that the next problem was to get the West African soldiers' home.

Agnes and Elizabeth were a little distracted, being more interested in a letter from home than in the meeting.

They did get to talk to the Indian doctor, who was confused when they spoke in unison. He was quickly back to normal, as he had seen identical twins before but not ones speaking in unison. They had a relative in India and Bertie had given them a lot of information about India. They had also seen Indian artefacts in Lionel's house. The new thing they learned from his brief address to the meeting was about tropical diseases. They promised to visit his ward in the near future. Lionel's son came to their mind and they hoped he would avoid all the symptoms the Indian doctor was telling them about.

The new letter from home had lots of news. Alice had taken Arthur to visit her parents. Benjamin had insisted on going with Arthur, so Elsie had gone with Alice to Leicestershire. Bertie had followed later to also stay; they were all having a good time. Alice's brother was always talking about the twins and in particular, praising them for designing his chair. Reggie's friend the General had talked him into visiting hospitals and talking about the twins. The general had told him he would be welcomed when he talked about his daughters. This was indeed the case; Matrons were asking him about news of his daughters. Old patients were asking when they would be back in England and new patients could not believe the stories they were hearing.

After breakfast one morning, Agnes was with Douglas while he was waiting to do his first operation. Being his first operation alone, he was awaiting some paperwork from the colonel and major. It was a formality but he knew the army was not keen on changes in its formalised system. Agnes said she would investigate. She went to the major's office, where he explained that he was awaiting the paper from the colonel. Then she went to the colonel's office to be told by his male secretary that the colonel was on an important phone call. She ignored the secretary, knocked on the door and walked into the colonel's office.

"Good morning, Agnes. I am trying to call England and we have a very bad line. What can I do for you?"

Agnes pointed to a paper on his desk and the colonel smiled and signed it.

"Sorry for the delay but I was trying to fix my wife's travel plans so she could visit me."

She thanked the colonel and took the paper to the major, who signed it and told her his wife was also coming to Egypt. Now the twins had a new topic of discussion: two middle-aged ladies, wives of high-ranking officers, coming to the hospital.

Douglas thanked her as she handed him the paper.

"I don't normally take liberties by entering the colonel's office without an invitation but I think we have earned a few indiscretions."

Agnes went back to her ward but decided she would have to apologise to the colonel at a later date. The major thanked her for taking initiative; he was off to see how Douglas was faring. Elizabeth came to congratulate her sister and tell her that the situation Douglas was in was worth a break in protocol. Agnes was in her ward later when there was some shouting coming from an incoming patient. He was a South African major who was protesting very loudly that, because of his rank, he wanted a separate room. Agnes tried to tell him there were no single rooms prepared as they were being renovated. That did not seem to quieten him down at all, so Agnes decided to give him the treatment. She mentally summoned her sister and soon they both faced the major and said he would get a single room when one was ready. He sat up on his bed with his mouth open and could not speak. A major in another bed said to a captain near him that for entertainment alone, he would rather be in this ward than locked up by himself in a room.

The South African major quieted down and the twins were then confronted by the engineering sergeant and a soldier arriving, pushing a wheelchair. He apologised that the modifications had taken longer than he expected but his whole team was excited about the finished product. He asked the twins to tell his soldier to get on a spare bed. Of course, after hearing them, the poor man stood stock still in shock until his sergeant told him these young ladies were scarier than any Turk. Even the South African major was laughing. (Later, the major personally apologised to Agnes for his earlier behaviour and said he wanted to stay on the ward.)

The soldier lay on the bed and the sergeant manoeuvred the wheelchair into place. He raised the seat, headrest and footrest to the correct height. He then pushed the tray to be flush with the bed. The twins took hold of the bedsheet and pulled the soldier into the wheelchair.

The whole ward erupted in clapping. At this point, the new matron entered the ward, accompanied by the colonel. They watched as the wheelchair was lowered into a normal position. The matron asked the colonel where they obtained such a contraption. He introduced her to the twins, declaring them to be engineers, nurses, entertainers and bloody good riders. The ward was in an uproar over this announcement and several of the bedridden officers wanted to try the wheelchair. The sergeant was shaking the twin's hands, totally forgetting all military protocols. He winked as he said they would make more but there were several military hospitals in Cairo and when word got out, his bridge-building days were over. This soldier's enthusiasm reminded the twins of the wheelchair builder in Leicester.

The new matron was a portly middle-aged lady from Melbourne who had a hard look about her but this was offset by a very good smile. The colonel told the twins they should meet back in his office after he had taken the matron on a tour of the whole hospital. Agnes thought that this meeting might not be the ideal time to apologise for entering his office without permission. Elizabeth ushered the matron and colonel into her ward. The twins had not yet treated the matron to the unison performance. From the soldier's ward, they went to the black soldier's ward and Elizabeth sensed some surprise from the matron. The black nurse (Njoki) talked to the matron with deference but also pointed out the difficulties the injured black soldiers were having. The colonel stayed quiet; he was going to promote her to her sister but had not yet completed the paperwork. The colonel's office was quite crowded with himself, the matron, two surgeons, two sisters, Captain John and the colonel's secretary. The colonel formally introduced the matron to all present. Of course, she had met everyone before but now it was her turn to speak.

"Well, at a cursory glance, I am happy this is a clean hospital. I have never lived in the desert before but I understand that sand can get everywhere. I know this place was a hotel before becoming a hospital but it is pleasing that there are large enough rooms to have decent size wards. One surprise was the ward for black soldiers but I will come back to that later. What surprised me was how cheerful most of the patients were. I went to the officer's ward to be greeted by smiling and laughing injured men. I went to the soldier's ward to find the same and even in the black soldier's ward, I saw smiling soldiers. I have been in many military hospitals where there were war veterans, generally from the Boer War but rarely got a smile. I have not yet seen the other wards and the operating theatre but I assume they will also be good. What perturbs me is why there is a black soldier's ward and why none of the soldiers there will talk to the sisters in charge."

The colonel interrupted at that point and said he would tell the matron of the history of the black soldiers' ward later. He wanted the senior sisters to tell them about the reason the black soldiers would not talk to them. He pointed to the twins, inviting them to talk.

"Matron, we know the problem but the nurse Njoki can explain it better than we can. May we call Njoki?"

They had spoken in unison and the matron sat back in her chair and said nothing. The officers in the room and the colonel's secretary had to suppress their laughter. The colonel had thought they would need Njoki and had arranged for her to be available; he was also going to confirm her promotion. She was waiting in the outer office.

The colonel asked his secretary to call Njoki. As she entered, she was thinking there was a problem.

The twins said, "Do not be afraid; these officers want to know why your soldiers will not talk to us. You are with friends here."

The colonel thought that their last remark was very good. In war, you needed friends, even more so if you were injured.

Njoki said, "When I met the sisters, I had seen identical twins but these ladies were so alike I could not tell the difference. When they talked in unison, I was in shock and it took me quite a time to recover my senses."

The colonel was having the same thoughts. Njoki went on to explain seeing double and how tonal languages were spoken. Everything was different in English.

The matron was still regaining her senses.

"If the sisters stand apart, the patients just keep looking from one to the other. I think they are more afraid of Nurse Agnes and Elizabeth than the whole Turkish army. The sisters have them bewitched; I think that is the word."

The colonel said, "Thank you, nurse and I am pleased to confirm that you have just been fully promoted to sister."

The matron had regained her senses and asked where Njoki was from.

"I am from near Nairobi; I am Kikuyu and I went to an English school in Nairobi."

"I want to thank you for that brief summary and I back the colonel's choice to promote you."

The colonel then dismissed the twins and Njoki. Outside the colonel's office, the twins were soon hugging Njoki and congratulating her on her promotion. Inside the colonel's office, he was explaining the history of the black soldiers' ward. Later that day, the twins were called to the matron's office. She said that she was not happy with a separate black soldier's ward. Her childhood had been in country Victoria, where she went to school with many Aboriginal boys and girls. So far, they have had no Aboriginal casualties. She had assumed there would be some but they had probably gone to other hospitals. The twins understood the problem and said any change should be slow. If they had an aboriginal casualty, they should put him in Elizabeth's ward with one or two new black patients. Elizabeth would make sure they were treated well and not subjected to the unison speech.

Later, Elizabeth was in her ward when a soldier came in on crutches with a large plaster of Paris on his leg. He was obviously Australian and was heading for the Australian contingent in the ward. Elizabeth asked him where he was going and in an expletive sentence, he told her. She did not bat an eyelid and mentally called her sister. They were going to give him the treatment.

"We see you are injured; was it by a bullet? And where did you come from?'

The whole ward was suppressing laughter. His Australian colleagues in arms were not going to help him one little bit.

After that initial shock, he explained that he had a broken leg and the surgeon said he could stay in the hospital for a few days. He was supposed to help around the wards in exchange for a comfortable bed. Elizabeth told him he should report to Captain John while she prepared a bed for him. The other Australian soldiers were telling Elizabeth to give him a hard time as he was a corporal; they apologised for his language.

The corporal came to John's office and told his story. He was from Queensland and had been riding horses all his life (Elizabeth was enjoying this part). They had landed at Suez and he was transferred to Cairo. He wanted to fight the Turks but there were none in Cairo. He had been to Brisbane and thought that all cities were basically the same but Cairo was a different city. It was dirty and full of dirty people. It was full of thieves and brothels. He then apologised to Elizabeth for talking about brothels. Elizabeth said she knew about brothels and John frowned at her remark. She gave him a wide smile and let the corporal carry on.

In telling his tale, this corporal recounted that he was with a group of soldiers in Cairo when they saw an Egyptian mistreating a horse pulling his cart. Now Elizabeth was on the corporal's side; mistreating horses had her angry and she could feel that Agnes was also angry in the next ward.

"This horse looked like he had been starved; you could see his ribs. We approached and started telling this guy he should be pulling his own cart. Now some of the locals surround us. As I approached the cart, I slipped in the mud and the cartwheel went over my leg. My mates pulled me out of there but that poor horse got no relief."

"I am glad I was not there; I might have shot the man."

The Australian corporal apologised for swearing when he first met Elizabeth and then inquired whether she had ever shot a gun?

"My sister and I have never shot a man but we have shot rabbits, a fox and plenty of pigeons."

Rabbits grabbed the corporal's attention.

"Rabbits are the curse of our land; some stupid buggers let some loose and now they are everywhere. None of our local animals can kill them and in some places, they are worse than the kangaroos. Some areas even have a bounty on rabbits and I understand some men are making a living shooting rabbits."

John was listening closely and although he thought there might not be any rabbits in Egypt there was a rifle range. He set about looking around the army camp outside the hospital grounds. With his wooden leg, he could walk fair distances. He realised he would need the commander's permission to use the range. The commander was a general and John had to leave a request with the general's secretary (a major). His request was to take a few of the medical staff to practise their shooting skills. The general's reply was that he was never sure whether medical people could shoot straight but he was happy to let them try.

John organised that he and Douglas would escort the twins to the rifle range. The surgeon said he would be an observer. Elizabeth was keen to get the Australian corporal to come along, ostensibly to load the weapons. This man had been talking to Elizabeth about hunting in Queensland. He loved to shoot rabbits and kangaroos. There were plenty of feral pigs and goats to shoot but they did not shoot koalas (the ladies did not like it and they were too easy targets). There were always snakes and goannas but further up north, there were crocodiles. He had never shot a crocodile. Elizabeth was amazed that they could just go out and shoot. It was so different in England.

The sergeant in charge of the rifle range was amazed when two nurses showed up to shoot. They said the Enfield three hundred three was heavy unless they were lying down and they did not want to lie in the sand. Elizabeth asked if he had two hundred two rifles. He produced two and Elizabeth sent off her first shot. It hit the outer bull and then the second shot did the same. The sergeant was watching a lady who could shoot. Elizabeth told Agnes there was something wrong with the rifle and could she borrow Agnes's rifle? This was all done with the audience in silence. Elizabeth took Agnes's gun and hit the bull with the next three shots. Agnes did the same with the next three shots. The first rifle obviously had a defect.

John had watched enough that he declined to shoot, as his leg was hurting. Douglas had a go and he hit the bull once. The corporal was watching and he declined to shoot; he could not bear the thought of being beaten by women. The sergeant in charge of the range was astounded but when the twins told him they had fun and thanked him for having them on his firing range, he was in another world. The major had witnessed everything. He had remained in the background.

The general in charge of the camp was not pleased that two nurses had shot well at his firing range. In his view, ladies had no business shooting rifles. He summoned the colonel to bring the nurses to his office. His first surprise was that he was seeing two identical ladies. They thanked him for inviting them to his office; their speech became his next surprise.

It took him a while to come to his senses. The colonel was enjoying a senior officer in strife.

"Please, tell me where you learned to shoot." It was the only thing that came to his mind.

"We were taught to shoot by our grandfather; our father was a brigadier fighting the Boers. He was not locked up in the towns but roved around in the veld, fighting the Boers. He told us the Boers were good shots and it was not until the British army took them seriously that they could be defeated."

The general became excited. "Was his name Reggie?"

"Yes, sir."

Now the general had risen from his desk and was throwing his arms in the air. Even the secretary looked surprised. The colonel took a step backwards and roared with laughter.

"He was my friend since the Zulu wars; he was my kind of soldier. I heard he had twins but I did not know they were beautiful young ladies. By Christ, this deserves a toast."

"Sorry, sir, we do not drink alcohol. Our father made us drink cider once but we did not like it."

They then told the story of the cider from Bromyard and the general was roaring with laughter. Young ladies who did not drink but could shoot were totally new to him. Identical twins who spoke in unison were very new to him and to his secretary.

"Oh, I would love to taste that cider and toast your father. I have not seen him since he resigned his commission."

"You should visit him on your next leave in England; you will be very welcome. He loves to see old army friends."

"Unfortunately, I will probably move nearer the front soon; I wish I had met you sooner. We could have talked more about your father and South Africa."

The colonel and general toasted Reggie with whisky and the twins drank water. After the meeting, the general's secretary told the colonel that initially the general was a bit annoyed by ladies shooting on the rifle range. That all changed when the twins spoke; he had never seen the general laugh so much. This general was not happy to be side-lined from the fight.

While the twins were with the general, a lieutenant had been admitted to Agnes's ward. He was an Australian. As Angela approached the man, she saw he was quite old. She engaged him in conversation and found he came from Newcastle, so she talked about coal. She was dying to ask about his age but he pre-empted her. He told her he was a sergeant during the Boer War but had been promoted to second lieutenant before coming to Egypt. A further promotion came on the battlefield but unfortunately, he had been shot in the leg. The British captain in the adjacent bed chimed in and said that the promotion of NCOs to officers was almost unheard of in the British army.

Agnes talked about the Zulu and Boer wars with this man. Elizabeth came in to listen and the lieutenant stopped talking. He said he had seen twins before but not identical ones. Agnes told him Elizabeth knew of their conversation about Newcastle, even though she had been in the other ward.

He said, "You are not fair dinkum; she must have been listening."

"We are fair dinkum."

Now the whole ward erupted in laughter and the lieutenant collapsed on his bed. It took him quite a while before he could speak.

"Never in my army career, never in my life have I ever met ladies like you; if I ever have children, you will be in all my stories."

The twins thought that was as good a comment as they had heard. This man became one of their favourite patients.

John was now doing very well getting around with his wooden leg and he said to Elizabeth that he wanted to see the Sphinx and the Pyramids. He felt he could ride with difficulty but Elizabeth advised she would find a sulky and she would let him drive. She talked Agnes into taking Douglas and two guards to look at the Sphinx. The guards pointed out that there was an encampment of locals close to the Sphinx and news about Arab affiliations had them wary of going too close. The guards were also being influenced by the stories from Cairo of thieving Egyptians.

They had three guards; the sergeant would ride with Agnes and Douglas and the other two would guard the sulky. They went fairly close to the Sphinx and John took out his binoculars. Then he surprised Elizabeth by producing a camera.

"Where did that come from?"

"I talked the colonel into getting a camera so we could show the war office a happy hospital. All the newspaper photographers are in the desert following the troops but they have labs in Cairo that can develop film. The colonel thought that his reports might look better with photographs."

At the Pyramids, John cajoled Elizabeth to stand with him, with the Pyramids in the background. Elizabeth was a bit bashful; she had never had her photograph taken before. John had an ulterior motive; he wanted to be seen with the most beautiful nurse in Egypt. Agnes and Douglas were having fun racing from one pyramid to the next and the sergeant was having fun keeping up.

The colonel was pleased with some of the photographs but he was not shown one of John and Elizabeth. His big personal news was that his wife had landed in Alexandria. The surgeon had the same news about his wife and the ladies were going to arrive together. The twins discussed army life for married couples and decided it may not be for them. They were starting to think about their age. In England, they might be considered old maids. Their father and uncle had never pushed them into marriage. As with every important decision, they wrote a list of the pros and cons. They decided nothing could be done until the war was over.

The wives arrived in Cairo and there was a whole troop as an escort for the carriages. The twins were in this convoy and they were seeing plenty of Cairo. Much of what they were seeing was not to their liking. Everyone was introduced at the railway station but Douglas was in the hospital holding the 'fort'. The colonel introduced everyone and left the twins until last.

"Please, sisters, greet my wife as only you can."

His wife looked at him with a frown.

"Welcome, ma'am. We think your husband is trying to embarrass you because when we are together, we speak this way and it has different effects on people. We think your husband is looking for your reaction."

After a few minutes, the colonel's wife told them that in all her years of marriage, she rarely found cause to reprimand her husband and she wouldn't be starting now. The colonel was in the background, laughing quietly. The major's wife was also in shock. John took a few photographs of the scene and then they were all off back to the hospital. The ladies were ensconced on the third floor; these were the best rooms and with the lift now working, they were very accessible. The twins fixed up a time to talk when the wives had settled in.

A message came from the general: he was leaving soon to join Allenby and push those Turks all the way back to Turkey. He wanted to have a leaving party and was inviting the twins, the colonel, his wife, the major and his wife. The general wanted to have some fun, so he asked the twins to come last so he could have his officers lined up to meet them. He greeted the twins at the door and asked them to speak to the officers.

"Good afternoon, gentlemen. We understand you are going east to join in the fight. Although we would wish to see you again, we do not wish to see you as casualties in our hospital."

There was silence and then the general started to roar with laughter.

"Thank you, my dears. I hope the Turks don't have the same effect on my troops."

Now the twins passed down the line, shaking each officer's hand. The officers were still in shock and said very little. The general took the twins to one side and ordered water for them. He had his whisky.

"I first met your father during the Zulu wars. He was in the cavalry and I was in the infantry. We were often nearly beaten by the Zulus but the cavalry just kept them at bay. I would often sit with your father and discuss the terrain. I was interested in using artillery and he was telling me about ground conditions. We both stayed in South Africa after the Zulu wars and then we were both involved in the Boer war. I was stuck in Ladysmith and your father was roaming the countryside. When we were relieved, I caught up with your father and he told me the British army's tactics of putting women and children in camps were not to his liking. I did not like it either but I had nothing to go back to if I resigned. Whereas your father had an estate and landed gentry family. I went to what is called a grammar school but all my colleagues went to public schools. My promotions came as I stayed in South Africa. At least we have Allenby to lead this campaign; he knew your father in South Africa. I am now a general but have been side-lined, probably because of my undistinguished family background. I am sorry if this is boring and sounds like sour grapes."

"No general, we are truly interested and a friend of our father has to be respected. We have always wondered, if our father had stayed in the army, whether he would have become a general. Of course, we are very glad he came home to run his estate."

"You ladies are a breath of fresh air. Well, anyway, I now have my chance to lead men into battle and decide on tactics. Wish me luck."

The general excused himself, as he had to talk to his other guests. The twins were hoping he came through the campaign alive and well and could visit their father on the estate. The next letter to their father and uncle was nearly all about the general. They always addressed their letters to their father and their uncle. Reggie did not mind, as he regarded Bertie as their second father.

Reggie was telling Bertie that maybe he should not have resigned his commission after the Boer War; he might now be a general. He then thought about the war in France and how useless the cavalry had been but the desert was another story. Bertie and Reggie were following every article about the war and Reggie was getting some inside information. The appointment of General Allenby to be in charge of fighting the Turks had Reggie in a very good mood; that man Allenby was going to have a positive influence on the war.

Alice and Elsie were wondering how the twins were coping with the heat. They wrote their own letters to the twins. Most of their letters were about the boys but they wondered about the injured officers. They also wondered about the dust (it was actually sand) from the desert.

Bertie had been made a member of the King's Council and was expecting to be made a judge soon. He had recently defended a couple of conscientious objectors, which had not made him popular with the public but the judiciary loved his courage. The twins thought that their uncle must believe these people were genuine and it made them think about war. They were seeing the results of the war but were wondering about what the nurses had to deal with in France. They often sat and talked about what it must be like in a field hospital. They were in a very comfortable hotel and hospital and could not imagine living in a tent. Although it was indeed hot in Egypt, they wondered if it was better or worse than the freezing rain in Belgium. On balance, they thought that they were in a better place.

The colonel knew that the twins had a great influence on the ground floor of the hospital but he was thinking he could perhaps use them on the second floor. The Indian doctor was very happy to have them visit his ward. Most of his patients would recover but he saw that a bit of entertainment could help things along. This was a welcome enough duty for the twins but they were at a loss for what to say to their captive audience. The Indian doctor told them their identical appearance and speech were important and it did not really matter what they said. The twins decided to talk to the patients about talking to animals. A whole ward hung on to their every word after the first shock of unison speech. The Indian doctor was full of praise; he had listened to every word. The twins had the whole ward talking and forgetting about their illnesses. On leaving, the twins told them all to get better and then go back to duty. One patient shouted that they would do that for the twins.

The next ward was the Venereal Disease Ward. This ward had seen a large increase in patients from Cairo. Many of the soldiers might recover but at the time, there was no known cure. The twins had seen VD at hospitals around Britain but particularly at the Mile End Road hospital. They were now confronted with a new dilemma: what would they say to these men? They decided to talk to one of the male nurses before going into the ward. This man was a conscientious objector but had chosen to act as a nurse. He was thinking that this service was almost worse than going to war. Of course, he was taken aback by the twins but he had been warned.

"Many of these men are ashamed of themselves but a few would do it again. Although I am an objector, I think you should tell them to get well and go and fight for their country."

"Thank you, nurse. We know our speech will have a shock effect but our advice might not have the same effect. We admire you for doing your job; it cannot be easy. May this war come to an end soon, so you can go home. We hope when you go home people will appreciate what you have done but we suspect that you will not get the praise that you deserve, so we give it to you from us."

"Thank you, sisters; actually, I might stay here in Egypt, where no one knows me. I am also not sure what reception I will get back in England."

The twins entered the ward to a few whistles and lots of chatter.

"Thank you, men. We know that many of you will recover but there is no cure for your disease. We want you all to recover and fight for your king and country."

The silence was almost deafening and so the twins produced a dominion flag and saluted it. They did not usually salute but it had the desired effect. Now they had men standing to salute the flag. The nurses and most of the patients were saluting and singing God Save the King.

It was all reported to the colonel and although this ward was against all his beliefs, the twins had shown their value once again. Bertie was rereading all the twins' letters and thinking about their long-dead mother, Sally; these were her babies and he was sure she would be very proud of them. The description of the VD ward and the male nurse brought a tear to his eye. He was not sure about the contentious objection but he had to defend any man who stood up for his beliefs. Reggie was not happy with the colonel, subjecting his daughters to talking to men he called cowards and malingerers. Although these brothers often had divergent views, they enjoyed each other's company and rarely quarrelled. On this subject, however, they agreed to differ; actually, they did that on many subjects.

John organised a trip to the pyramids for the wives. The colonel's wife and the major's wife would be in a sulky, driven by a sergeant. There would be three soldiers guarding this sulky. John and Elizabeth would be in another sulky. Agnes and Douglas would be with their favourite sergeant and would ride freely. The ladies wanted to see the Sphinx and the Pyramids, so the sulkies went as close as the guards wanted to go. It was early but one man came out on his donkey. According to the guards, he was using very bad language towards the sulkies. The wives did not understand but the man was showing aggression.

Agnes asked the corporal whether she could borrow his rifle.

"I hope you are not going to shoot him."

"No, I just want to give him a scare."

Elizabeth said to John that her sister was going to shoot a handkerchief.

"I see no handkerchief."

"Just wait and see."

Agnes rode up, assessed the situation and rode towards the man on his donkey. She rode past him and dropped a handkerchief, then turned the horse and shot the handkerchief. Then she pointed the rifle at the man. A donkey, at full speed, was soon seen disappearing into the desert. The wives were watching in awe; although they were military wives, this was women firing at a target. The whole group was in awe. The pyramids were impressive but all they could talk about was a handkerchief shot from a horse. The sergeant kept repeating to himself, "They can shoot as well as ride."

John said, "You knew that she was going to shoot the hanky before it happened?"

"Yes, I was telling my sister it was a good idea. One problem is we have no privacy from each other and I think it will not change until we perhaps have a long separation."

"If I had a brother, I am not sure whether I would like him knowing my every thought."

"For us, it is a fact of life."

John was in love with Elizabeth but could only tell it was her by the lack of a badge. He had been told about Benjamin and thought there must be some difference. He studied their faces a lot, trying not to stare. He looked at their ears, noses and eyebrows and could see no difference. They both had the same smell and he could not detect any difference in their walk. He was trying to look at their whole bodies and finally came to their hands. He had held Elizabeth's hands several times but never held Agnes's hands. He got the chance when he took their photograph together. He persuaded them to put their hands up as if in surrender; he was telling them it was a joke. They complied, going along with the joke. John was telling them to send a photograph to their father. He studied this photograph with a magnifying glass and found the index finger on Agnes's right hand was bent. Now he had the identification secret he needed. He wondered whether Benjamin used that finger to identify them. They had surely both held his hands.

The colonel was very happy with the trip to the pyramids but now he had a different problem looming. He called Agnes to his office and explained she would be receiving an Indian officer in her ward and this man was a Muslim. Agnes said they would accommodate his every need if it were possible. The colonel said that he would be watching this situation.

The Indian lieutenant was wheeled into the ward. He had been shot in the abdomen. Agnes attempted to talk to him but the man was silent. She then decided to pull rank and said he was still in the army and that she would expect answers to her questions. The man was wide-eyed but realised he should answer questions.

"Tell me, what are your requirements?"

The whole ward was quiet.

"Well, I need to pray five times a day and the first one is at four a.m. I cannot eat pork or drink alcohol. I want a male nurse and when I pray, I must be facing east towards Mecca."

"Thank you, lieutenant. We have a special wheelchair that will not be in use at four a.m. We will have to instruct the night nurses regarding the positioning but I am afraid that you will not be able to get on your knees to pray. We rarely get pork and alcohol is banned for the patients, even though that is not a popular rule for most of our patients. The problem is a male nurse; we have only female nurses on this ward. I think the best you can do is imagine the nurse giving you a wash, being your mother or wife."

"Well, sister, I have no wife but I do have a mother and I will close my eyes and think of her."

"Where are you from in India?"

"I come from East Bengal, near Dacca. My father is a preacher and did not want me to join the army. I went to an English school and that got me into the officer corps. We lived on a farm and had buffalo."

"Do you talk to the animals?"

The lieutenant frowned and did not reply; he thought it was a strange question.

Agnes then started to tell him about her father's estate and how they treated the animals. He was still frowning, so Agnes said she was a poor liar but her story would be confirmed by her sister.

"Where is your sister?"

"In the next ward, I will summon her."

The lieutenant watched and Agnes did not say a word and Elizabeth duly appeared.

"I understand the lieutenant from West Bengal is sceptical about our talking to animals."

The rest of the room was holding back laughter. The lieutenant was speechless, so they thought they would give him the treatment.

"We understand India is a very large country with millions of people. Our uncle told us a little about Gandhi. We understand he is Hindu but he is trying to do good for all Indians and he supports the British in this war. What do you think?"

The lieutenant sat for a couple of minutes and finally said, "It is a very complex subject that I cannot discuss in this condition, as I am still in a trance."

The twins apologised and said they had taken advantage and would not do that again. All the lieutenant could do was lie back on his bed and stare at the ceiling. Agnes found the Indian doctor and asked whether he would have a word with the lieutenant.

Their next letter home had a lot about the handkerchief incident and the Indian lieutenant. They could not say much about the war but it looked like Allenby was pushing the Turks back. They had heard something about Major Lawrence out in the desert but most of the officers and soldiers did not trust the Arabs, so this story seemed far-fetched. They had seen Cairo and were glad they were outside, near the pyramids. They were intrigued by stories about India from the doctor and the Muslim lieutenant. They wondered whether they should go there after the war.

In reply to Alice and Elise's letters, they said that the hospital was airy and that having fans was just bearable. Although the day could be hot, the nights could be cool and many nurses preferred the night shift. Fine sand was everywhere and any clean surface was covered in minutes. When they had a sandstorm called a haboob, they had to shut all the windows and doors and still the sand got inside. The nurses were continually cleaning and trying to keep the hospital sterile.

They missed small children and were always thinking of Benjamin and Arthur. They did not know how long the war would last but they could not leave before the end of the war. It was their hope that the boys were not too grown up before they saw them.

The colonel was getting glowing reports from the War Office. Apparently, a secret inspection of the hospital had been carried out and the inspectors had reported that they had never seen so many laughing patients. The colonel was a bit perturbed that there was an inspection done in secret. He called the twins, the matron and the surgeon major to his office.

"I have a report from the war office. They apparently did a secret inspection, which we passed but who were these inspectors?"

The major said he had a visit from the quartermaster's office, asking whether he had enough equipment. He did a tour of the operating room and then went to see the Indian doctor. The matron said no officer had approached her. Agnes said the black soldier ward was visited by a lieutenant from the Gold Coast. She had a talk with him about why the soldiers would not talk to her. According to Njoki, they told him about my sister and me; it was all very complimentary. I have many officers visiting my other ward and I could not pick out any one visitor who may have been a spy. Elizabeth said one Australian officer had visited her ward but he told his countrymen they were going home. There was a sergeant who talked to some of the soldiers but he did not look like a spy.

"This report was quite lengthy but the major conclusion was that a hospital with laughing injured soldiers must have been doing something correctly."

After this meeting, the twins conferred and they tried to pinpoint the identities of the inspectors. They could not and that worried them. It was possible one of Agnes's patients was the spy.

The war was going well in Palestine but there was chaos in Cairo. There were more VD cases and more broken limbs. Apparently, there had been several riots in Cairo and even fighting among soldiers. Finally, after all their discussions, one Aboriginal soldier was admitted and the matron could use this to admit black soldiers to Elizabeth's ward. The matron came personally to talk to the man and Elizabeth accompanied her. This man was from Sydney and Elizabeth told him what she knew about Sydney. He had a white father and an aboriginal mother and that was why he was let into the army. The matron left them to it. He told her he was from La Perouse and she told him that was the name of a French admiral. Bertie's teaching was reaping rewards. The other black soldiers were talking to Elizabeth, as they had not been treated to the unison speak.

The matron called Elizabeth to her office.

"I want you to be careful with this man; he reminds me of my school days. I don't want you to give him any liberties as such but give him some leeway."

"Matron, he is a soldier like any other I treat. I will listen to what he says and act accordingly. If there is a problem, I will consult you but so far, so good."

The matron was pleased with Elizabeth's approach.

The West African wounded soldiers were a problem because there seemed no way of getting them home but John went to Alexandria to find out if there were any freighters travelling down the west coast of Africa. He found, to his delight, that they could get to Gibraltar, then join a hospital ship going to South Africa, then be dropped off in Accra and Lagos. He organised for Njoki to take her patients to Alexandria to see them comfortably on a freighter. Njoki was very pleased and even gave John a hug (in private). The soldiers chosen were very happy and there was an outbreak of joyful singing in their ward.

Douglas and the major were getting men with more complicated injuries shipped back from the front. The field hospitals were always on the move and could only give preliminary treatment to some of the badly wounded. The surgeons found that now they did not have any time to ride out to the Pyramids. Agnes and Elizabeth were also seeing an increasing workload. They actually spent one day a week on the night shift.

All the news from the front was good and that cheered up many of the officers and soldiers. All the talk was about the Allies taking Jerusalem and Damascus and the Muslim officer told Agnes that Jerusalem had a large mosque and was regarded as a holy city for his religion. Agnes was learning a lot about the Muslim religion and this officer was learning to relax among women. Much of the talk in the officer's ward was about the war in Europe. In the soldiers' ward, it was about the war in Palestine and Syria; that was a happier situation. The officers seemed to be more interested in the war and the soldiers were more interested in getting home.

The twins had written to the matrons in Birmingham and Mile End Road. They had described their hospital and staffing, although they could say little about the patients. The Birmingham matron had replied that her hospital was fully staffed; many nurses did not want to go to Europe. There were some bad stories about hospitals in Belgium and France. The Matron from Mile End Road was short-staffed and she had written to the War Office to get more staff. There was no reply, so she said that she was going to write directly to the twin's administrator and matron. Initially, there had been many volunteer nurses but information about the true conditions in Europe had leaked out and very few ladies wanted to see the carnage.

The colonel called the matron to his office; he had received a letter from the military hospital in London requesting nurses. The matron said that she had also received a similar letter. They called the twins to the office, as their military records showed that they had spent time in the London Military Hospital. The colonel said that as the administrator; he had the power to send a nurse for training in England but it was up to the nurse's organisation to allow a transfer.

The matron agreed that a hospital under stress was a place where they should help. The twins apologised as they had perhaps created this situation when they had written to the matron in London. They said that any nurse going to England would get new experience and that could only benefit the army. They suggested Njoki was already a very experienced nurse but this potential experience could only benefit her. The East End of London had many black people and she would not be totally out of place. Njoki was to be asked if she would like to go to London.

Njoki confronted Elizabeth soon after this and asked if she had recommended her to go to London. Elizabeth started to reply that the twins had written to their old matron. Before she could finish, Njoki was kissing her and thanking her for this opportunity. Agnes was enjoying the kissing (second hand) and the thought of travelling to London. All the other nurses were rejoicing at Njoki's good luck. The colonel wished to have another secret inspection so that the powers in charge could receive another report of happy nurses and patients. He also had two happy female visitors. Njoki told the black ward patients her news and they were singing and clapping. One of the patients asked Njoki if she could get Elizabeth; he would try to talk to her.

"I have been told to talk for the patients of this ward. First, let me introduce myself. I am Jacob from the north of the Gold Coast; Jacob is my Christian name but I have other local names. I spent a few years in a missionary school. We are sorry that most of us cannot talk to you but identical twins to us are like magic and when you speak together, we are bewitched, a word Njoki taught me. With all that, we are very happy that you treat us so well. This hospital is so clean and even though we want to go home, we cannot look forward to anything like this. We have thanked Captain John for getting our West African soldiers on their way home. Now we want to thank you and your sister for allowing Njoki to go to London. She will have an opportunity none of us could see in our future. Even if you are witches, you are good ones."

Elizabeth wanted to properly thank Jacob but all she could say was "thank you." Her emotions got the better of her. Agnes was in the next ward, crying.

There were plenty of good reports coming back from the front (the Middle Eastern one, not the European) and the matron would read the news that was allowed, first to the officers and then to the soldiers. Several of the soldiers told Elizabeth that the matron reminded many of them of their mothers. That set the twins thinking of their mother and whether one day they would be themselves mothers.

The colonel called the senior staff to a meeting, where he announced that Jerusalem had been captured. He admitted that it was of little military significance but politically and psychologically, it was a great boost for Britain and a large feather in Allenby's cap. Later, he told them that Damascus had been taken and General Chauvel had entered the city to appoint the governor. When he announced that in the soldier's ward, there was a large cheer section of Australian soldiers. The colonel viewed the taking of Damascus as a more important military victory, as it was close to the Turkish border. He decided he would put a map on a board and exhibit in all the wards. This was a great success.

There were more visitors than ever before, particularly to the soldier's ward and the matron had to set visiting hours. Many of the visitors were upset that alcohol was prohibited in the wards. One particularly obstinate visitor would not give up his bottle. Elizabeth called Agnes and in unison, they told him *no alcohol*! The man stood open-mouthed and they took his bottle without protest. The whole ward was in an uproar. Agnes was berating the officers whose friends brought alcohol; it was setting a bad example for the soldiers. Some of the patients were allowed in the courtyard but the twins warned them that any drunken men would be made to sleep outside overnight. It was a mark of respect that no soldier or officer slept outside overnight.

The twins wrote home that when the war ended, they would stay as long as needed but then they had a plan. Agnes would propose marriage to Douglas and Elizabeth would propose marriage to John.

When Reggie read this, he was astounded; Bertie was laughing.

"Our father predicted the future and your daughters are the future."

Printed in the USA
CPSIA information can be obtained
at www.ICGtesting.com
CBHW030407270824
13760CB00008B/358